5

A DIXIE MORRIS ANIMAL ADVENTURE

GILBERT MORRIS

MOODY PRESS
CHICAGO

To Andrea—
I love you very much.
We were sisters;
now we are friends.
Dixie Lynn

All Scripture quotations, unless indicated, are taken from the *New American Standard Bible,* © 1960, 1962, 1963, 1968, 1971, 1972, 1973, 1975, 1977, and 1994 by The Lockman Foundation, La Habra, Calif. Used by permission.

ISBN: 0-8024-3376-7

1 3 5 7 9 10 8 6 4 2

Printed in the United States of America

CONTENTS

1
HOME AGAIN

Dixie Morris came out of a sound sleep and for a moment did not know where she was. Quickly opening her eyes, she was relieved to see that she was in her own bed in the Airstream trailer she shared with Aunt Sarah. She let her eyes run over the familiar sights and drew a deep sigh of relief. Sometimes she still woke up in the morning thinking she was in a desert tent far across the ocean.

"I had a good time over in the Middle East," she murmured to the Barbie doll lying beside her on the pillow, "but I'm glad to be home again."

She picked up the doll—it was named Scarlett after Scarlett O'Hara in the book *Gone with the Wind*. She smoothed down its gorgeous dress and, as she often did, began talking to the Barbie.

"It's good to see you again, Scarlett," she murmured. "I've got to tell you about Sandy, the camel. He was my friend on our trip to the desert. And now Sandy and five other camels have come to join the circus."

Dixie smoothed the doll's hair back from its face and lowered her voice. She remembered that Aunt Sarah would be still asleep, only a few feet away in her own bed toward the front of the trailer, and Dixie did not want to awaken her. "I didn't like Sandy at first because a camel spit on me when I first got there. But he was so sweet, and he saved my life, too."

She went on to whisper the story of how she and Aunt Sarah had made friends with the family of Aimee Feyd, a young woman they had met and befriended. She told the doll how they had gone on a trip to Aimee's country and met the girl's family. And she told about the wonderful adventure she'd had there.

"But I'm glad to be home, Scarlett. I've missed you."

Placing the doll back on the pillow, Dixie threw back the covers and got out of bed. Quickly and quietly she washed her face, brushed her teeth, and then stood wondering what to wear. She finally picked out a pair of white shorts that she had bought at The Limited, a lime green shirt, and a pair of brown sandals. When she was dressed, she went into the kitchen area where she found Aunt Sarah just beginning to stir.

"You go get dressed, Aunt Sarah," Dixie said, "and I'll fix us breakfast."

Sarah Logan, aged twenty-two, pushed her red hair out of her eyes and smiled. She had bright green eyes, and Dixie thought she was very attractive, even when she first woke up!

"That'll be good, Dixie. I think I still have jet lag even after all this time."

After her aunt had gone into the bathroom and the water started running in the shower, Dixie began preparing breakfast. She'd decided on pancakes. First, she took down a large glass bowl from the cupboard, then measured two cups of pancake mix. She poured them into the bowl, added milk, and then two eggs. With a large wooden spoon from the wall in front of her, Dixie began to beat the batter until it was smooth and thick. When the griddle was heated, Dixie poured spoonfuls of batter into it.

Next, while the first pancakes cooked, she put some turkey bacon into the microwave and started Aunt Sarah's coffee in the Mr. Coffee machine.

Her aunt came out just as everything was ready. She had put on an old robe that she had had for years, and she was barefoot. "Nice to be waited on," she said. She smiled at Dixie as she sat down. "This is better than the nicest restaurant in the world."

Dixie was pleased, for she liked to do things for Aunt Sarah. The two bowed their heads, and Dixie asked the blessing. When she looked up, she said, "Are you glad to be back in the States, Aunt Sarah?"

"Yes! Those long, overseas trips tire me, and it's always good to be home. This trailer looks better to me than a palace."

They ate a leisurely breakfast. Aunt Sarah liked maple syrup on her stack of pancakes, but Dixie had discovered Louisiana sorghum. It was very dark, and Aunt Sarah shuddered as Dixie poured it over hers.

"That's looks like old motor oil!" she exclaimed. "How can you ever eat it?"

"It's good!" Dixie said firmly. "You ought to try it."

After breakfast, Dixie got up and went straight to their small freezer. She took out a little box and was opening it when Aunt Sarah went by with her hands full of dirty dishes. She stopped to look over Dixie's shoulder.

"And what's that?" she asked.

"Chicken livers."

"I don't want any chicken livers."

"It's not for you. It's for Stripes."

Sarah put the dishes in the sink, then tousled Dixie's long blonde hair. "I might have known that you'd be back to taking care of that tiger," she said.

"He's my best friend—best animal friend, that is."

While the livers were thawing, Dixie played with her Nintendo game. She had a brand-new one that was more fun than any of her old Nintendos.

Aunt Sarah left in the middle of the game. She was the veterinarian for the Royal Circus and was kept busy all day every day with the many animals.

When the livers were thawed, Dixie fried them, and their good smell filled the small trailer. Then she put the cooled livers into a plastic bag and went outside.

She had to blink at the bright sunlight that shone in her face. "But it's not as hot here in Florida as it was in the desert," she said to herself. "And I'm glad for that!" The circus was in Miami that week. Dixie hoped she could go to the beach while they were there.

Going through the menagerie tent, she passed by Ruth, the elephant she always rode in the opening parade. Dixie stopped long enough to reach into her pocket and give Ruth an apple she had cut into quarters.

"There you go, Ruth. There'll be more later, sweetheart," she said and patted the elephant's rough brown trunk.

Gently Ruth put her trunk around Dixie and gave her a little hug.

"I've got to go now. I'll see you at the Spec." Why the opening parades were called Specs, Dixie never understood.

She passed a group of clowns practicing their act. They were using a mule whose one talent was to buck and stubbornly refuse to go anywhere. She stopped and said to one of them, "What's the matter, Bigg? Can't you make her go?"

Bigg was really Russell Hamilton Bigg. He was a midget who had become one of Dixie's best friends. He came over and gave her a good-morning hug.

Dixie felt odd hugging an adult who was shorter than she was, but she liked Bigg very much and hugged him back.

"Good to have you back from your desert trip. Did you really have as good a time as I hear?" the clown asked.

"Oh, yes, it was fine, Bigg. And those trained camels are so neat."

"I still don't think much of camels. I hear they spit at you."

Dixie laughed. "They do! One camel spit right at me. I found out you just have to know how to get along with them."

Bigg lifted his clown hat politely and said, "Thank you, but no thanks. I'll stick with Irene." Irene was Bigg's trained mule. "You want to ride Irene?" he asked.

"No. She doesn't go anywhere. I'm going to take Stripes these chicken livers. You want one?"

Bigg stared at the golden fried liver, but he shook his head. "No, thanks. I'd rather have a chocolate soda."

"So would I, but Stripes likes chicken livers. See you later, Bigg."

Dixie continued on her way to the cage where the powerful tigers were kept. One of them was resting against the bars of the cage. He was a Siberian tiger and was almost white. When Dixie spoke to him, he turned his huge head toward her, opened his eyes wide, and began to rumble deep in his chest. Then he got to his feet and shoved his head against the bars.

Dixie rubbed his head and whispered to him, saying sweet things and feeding him the chicken livers he loved.

While she was still talking to the tiger, a voice said, "Hey, Dix!" and she turned to see Mickey Sullivan coming across the menagerie tent toward her.

Mickey was her best friend. He was the son of Mooey and Irene Sullivan, the two who did the elephant act. Mickey was ten years old, Dixie's age. He had flaming red hair and bright blue eyes. "It's just like old times to have you back," he said when he came up.

"Seems that way to me too."

Mickey was rather shy about some things. She knew he was truly glad to see his friend back but did not quite know how to express his pleasure.

"But it sounds like you had a wild time over there," he added.

"You come on back to the trailer, and I'll tell you more about the desert. We've got some pancakes left over, too, if you want them."

Mickey's eyes brightened. "Do I want pancakes? Lead me to 'em!"

Fifteen minutes later, he was washing down the last of his pancakes with big swallows of milk. "Boy," he said, "those were the best pancakes in the world! You're some cook, Dixie."

"Well, Aunt Sarah's a good cook, and she's teaching me. So is Miss Clara."

"Now tell me more about the camel race and the sandstorm and getting lost and . . ."

They went back to the living room section and sat down. Dixie, as usual, was holding Scarlett, and Mickey, with his legs crossed and his hands behind his head, leaned back on the couch. He listened until Dixie had finished and then said, "Boy, that was some trip. I was surprised about those trained camels, though. I thought camels were too dumb to learn anything."

"No, camels can be real smart. They're stubborn, though. If they decide they have too much weight on them, they just won't move."

Mickey grinned. "That's being smart. If I was a camel, that's what I would do."

"Now it's your turn," Dixie said. "We've all been so busy there's hardly been time to talk since we got back. Tell me what else happened at the circus while I was gone."

Mickey made himself comfortable by lying flat on his stomach and placing his chin on the palms of his hands. "Well," he said, "you missed the wedding."

"I know about that. Mia and Kirk got married. I'm sorry I missed that."

"Yeah. You should have been here."

Mia Marino was a flyer with the circus. Kirk Delaney was one of the lion and tiger tamers. Dixie had wanted so much to be in their wedding.

"Mia still wanted you to be a flower girl. They had the wedding in a church with everything—all the trimmings. You should have seen it."

"What else has happened?"

"Well, Eric is as big a nerd as ever."

Eric. The pesky son of the Von Bulows.

They did an act with several fine Arabian horses.

"What about Darla?"

Mickey closed his eyes. "Oh, wow! Why do you have to ask about *her?*"

"So what's she done now?"

Darla Castle had been a problem for Dixie from the time they met. She was the prettiest girl Dixie had ever seen, but she was spoiled to the bone. She was the daughter of the Flying Castles, who did a high wire act. Darla was already in the act, and she didn't think that anybody who wasn't circus back for a hundred years amounted to much. Dixie had tried to be friends with her, but it was really hard.

"Darla's just being Darla—a nerdette, I guess," Mickey said. "I'd sure hate to be the guy that marries her. She's a pain in the neck!"

"Maybe it'll be you!" Dixie grinned. She liked to tease Mickey about Darla, for when the pretty girl had first come to the circus, Mickey had been dazzled by her. It almost ruined their friendship. But he eventually learned that Darla was not a girl that anyone would want to spend a lot of time with.

"She's pretty, but she's a real pain!" he announced. "Oh, and I forgot to tell you! There's going to be a new act."

"What kind of act?"

"Trained bears. Supposed to be really something. They'll get here tomorrow. Now, let's play Monopoly."

They got out the Monopoly board and soon were engaged in trying to stay out of jail and passing Go to collect two hundred dollars.

As usual, Mickey enjoyed the game hugely. The only problem was that he hated to lose, so Dixie—who didn't care whether she won at Monopoly or not—usually managed to let him win. She looked across at his beaming face after he had won yet another game, and she thought, *Well, it's fun to travel, but it sure is good to be home again.*

2
WELCOMING
COMMITTEE

Dixie discovered that the trip to the Middle East had tired her out more than she knew. Sometimes she stayed sleepy all day and went to bed right after supper.

She actually missed breakfast one morning and got up about eleven o'clock. She had just zipped herself into a pair of Levi's and pulled a blue T-shirt over her head when she heard the door slam. Dixie went out into the living area and found Aunt Sarah, who had brought back a sack that said "Taco Bell" on it.

"Oh, good! Taco Bell for lunch! I've missed my Taco Bell stuff!" Dixie beamed.

The two sat down and filled up on spicy tacos, a Coke for Aunt Sarah, and milk for Dixie.

"I just came from meeting the stars of the newest act," her aunt said.

"You mean the bears?"

"Yes. And they're beautiful animals."

"How many are there?"

"Just two." Sarah took a sip of her Coke. "They're as big as Stripes, I think. In fact, they're rather frightening to look at."

"Are they dangerous?"

"Any animal *that* big can be dangerous, but they seem to be very tame."

"How about the people?"

"I only met the man. His name is Gregori Malkovitch."

"Gregori *what?*"

"It's a Russian name." Aunt Sarah smiled. "They haven't been in this country too long, so Mr. Malkovitch speaks with a strong accent. His English is very good, though."

"Does he have a family?"

"He's a widower, but he has two children. A boy and a girl."

"How old are they?"

"I don't know. They weren't there. But you'll meet them soon enough. As a matter of fact," she said, "why don't you go over and invite them all to church tomorrow?

20

We must be polite to the new members of our circus family."

The church did not meet in a building with a steeple. The people met in the Big Top, and Mooey Sullivan, the elephant trainer, was the preacher. Every Sunday morning, many of the circus performers and workers met for a brief service. Aunt Sarah had begun teaching a Sunday school class for all the boys and girls, too.

"They're probably Greek Orthodox," she said, "but it would be nice if they would come."

"What's Greek Orthodox?"

"It's the largest religious group in Russia."

"Oh. Well, I'll go over right now."

"I wish we had some fresh bread or cookies for you to take to them. People always did that when I was growing up," Aunt Sarah said. "When a new family moved in, all the neighbors would come bringing a little something. Fresh bread or a jar of homemade pickles or—"

"I know! I'll bake them some brownies!"

"Oh, that would be nice! I'm sure the children would like them. But they may be older than you. Mr. Malkovitch isn't a young man, so his children may be older."

21

"Then they might even be grown up!" Dixie was disappointed, for she was always looking for new friends.

"Well, no matter how old they are, they'll like your brownies. I've got to go see the Calenties' dogs now. One of them has a cold or something."

As soon as her aunt left, Dixie began making the brownies. She loved to cook and was always experimenting.

"I'd better use my old recipe," she muttered as she went over to the cabinet.

She took down her recipe file and turned on the small oven to 350 degrees. Then she measured one cup of butter into a large saucepan and added four squares of unsweetened chocolate. She put the mixture over medium heat, stirring it occasionally, and waited patiently until the butter melted.

Dixie then measured two cups of sugar, one and one-half cups of flour, four eggs, one teaspoon of salt, one teaspoon of baking soda, and two teaspoons of vanilla, and added all these ingredients to the saucepan.

She stirred the mixture with a wooden spoon for about four minutes, then gently folded in one cup of chocolate chips. Finally, Dixie greased a baking pan, poured in the batter, and placed it in the oven.

When the brownies were done and Dixie took them out of the oven, she looked at her work with satisfaction. "You look good," she said, "but I'd better try one of you to be sure." She cut them into squares and carefully lifted one out. She tasted it and nodded. "If I do say so myself, I make the best brownies in the world." She suddenly looked up and said, "Lord, I don't want to be proud, but these are good brownies. I believe even You would like them."

She put some of the cooled brownies on a paper plate, wrapped aluminum foil over the top, and left the Airstream. She had been with the circus long enough to know the trailers of all the performers, and across the lot was a trailer she didn't know.

Dixie stopped Sidney Lo, the juggler. She asked, "Mr. Lo, is that where the new people live? The Malkovitches?"

"Sure is, Dixie. Good to see you back. Wani's been lost without you." Wani was his eleven-year-old daughter and one of Dixie's best friends.

"Tell her we'll get together tonight at our trailer."

"She'll be glad to hear that."

Dixie walked up to the small step of the new trailer and knocked on the door. But no one answered. She began to think that no one was home and was about to leave.

But just as she turned to go away, a little girl came around the corner of the trailer. She was no more than six, Dixie thought, and she was wearing a *dress*. That was unusual. Most circus people wore shorts or jeans.

"Hello, my name is Dixie Morris. I've come to welcome you to the circus."

The girl had long reddish blonde hair tied up in a ponytail. Her eyes were dark blue. She looked pretty, except for the rather ugly dress, and she did not smile, as Dixie expected her to do.

When the girl said nothing, Dixie grew rather embarrassed. "Well," she said, "welcome to the Royal Circus." When the girl still said nothing, Dixie stepped toward her and held out the plateful of brownies. "Here, I've baked these as a welcoming gift."

The little girl just stared at her. She appeared to be a little frightened, but perhaps she was just shy.

At that moment the trailer door opened, and a boy came out. He was tall and thin and looked to be close to Dixie's own age. His light brown hair fell down over his eyes, and he had a frown on his face. "What do you want?" he said.

Dixie swallowed, for he was not polite. "I'm Dixie Morris," she said. "My Aunt Sarah is the veterinarian for the circus." When the boy did not respond, she said, "She saw your bears yesterday. She said they're beautiful." Still the boy did not say anything. Dixie was getting very flustered. "Here," she said, thrusting the plate toward him. "This is to welcome you."

The boy stared at the covered paper plate, then slowly reached out to take it. "What is it?" he muttered. He had an accent of some kind.

"They're brownies," she said. "I made them myself."

The boy gaped at her, then lifted a corner of the foil. Then he reached inside, took one, and handed it to the little girl. She took a big bite, then held out her hand for more. He gave her another, then bit off half a brownie himself.

Just then a big man came around the

corner of the trailer. "Who is this?" he demanded in a booming voice.

"She brought us cake. Her name is Dixie Morris. Her aunt is the veterinarian."

"*Da.* Miss Logan." He looked Dixie up and down. He was very tall and strongly built. He had a head of bushy reddish hair and a thick beard.

He was looking at Dixie so strangely that she grew embarrassed. "Well, I just came over to welcome you to the circus."

"My name is Malkovitch. These are my children, David and Katherine—we call Katy."

"I'm glad to see you with the circus," Dixie said. She smiled at Katy then. "You'll have a good time here. There are some nice kids." When the girl did not respond, she turned to David. "We have Sunday school tomorrow morning. My aunt teaches the lesson. I wish you'd come." She looked up and said, "And you too, Mr. Malkovitch."

Gregori Malkovitch's eyes narrowed. Dixie could see his mouth turn down, even behind his beard. He said, "Ve do not go to church."

"Oh," Dixie said, disappointment in her voice. "Well, at least you can come over and visit us sometime."

"Ve do not visit."

Dixie swallowed hard. All three Malkovitches kept looking at her as if she had come from another planet or as if she had come to collect a bill. "Well," she muttered, "welcome to the circus, anyway."

Back in the Airstream, Aunt Sarah was working on her records, but she listened to Dixie tell of her visit to the Malkovitch trailer.

"I don't know what's the matter with those people. They took the brownies and didn't even say thank you. And when I asked them to church, Mr. Malkovitch just said, 'Ve don't go to church!'"

"That's too bad," her aunt said sympathetically. "But they're new to this country."

"That's no excuse for bad manners."

"It might be—a little bit," Aunt Sarah mused. She nibbled on the eraser of her pencil. She had the habit of nibbling erasers until there was none left. Fortunately she did not make many mistakes!

"Be very nice to them, Dixie," she said finally. "They probably need friends."

"I *was* nice, but they weren't polite!"

"When people are angry or not friendly, they're usually unhappy about something," Aunt Sarah said. "I'll tell you what. Let's you and I just be extra nice to the Malkovitches."

Dixie frowned. "Well, I'll try," she said, "but it's hard to be nice to somebody who's biting your head off all the time."

"Mr. Malkovitch's bark is probably worse than his bite."

"Well, I'd rather be bitten once than barked at all the time."

Aunt Sarah laughed. She gave Dixie a hug. "You mind what I say. We'll be as nice to the Malkovitches as we can."

3

THE STRANGE STRANGERS

To Dixie, one of the most exciting parts of the circus was the Spec—the opening parade. From the time she and her aunt had first joined the circus, they had taken part in it. Way back then, Bigg had told them, "We get everybody we can in the Spec —to make it look more impressive. So get used to it."

Dixie had become accustomed to the timing of the circus, too. The afternoon performance was always at one o'clock, and the evening performance was at seven. It seemed that most of her life revolved around those three events.

As the hands of the clock moved toward another Spec time, Dixie got into her costume. It was a harem girl outfit with a top and bottom like a modest two-piece swimsuit, and a filmy top and bottom that went on over that, down to her wrists and ankles. Quickly she pinned up her long hair and placed a veil over her face. The shoes she wore were specially made with toes that turned up in a funny curl. She put them on and started for where the parade was forming.

On the way she met Wani Lo, the oriental girl who was both a contortionist and an acrobat. "Hi, Wani."

"Hello, Dixie." Wani was wearing a silver body suit with imitation jewels all over it. Suddenly she bent over backward and put her head between her ankles as easily as Dixie could eat ice cream.

"I don't see how you ever do that!" Dixie exclaimed. "Don't you have any bones?"

"Sure, I got bones! They just bend easy." Wani grinned up at her. She seemed to tie herself in a knot, then stood upright. "That sure is a pretty costume. Blue is really your color."

"Thank you, Wani. You look nice, too." She looked around and said, "I don't see the bears and the Malkovitches."

Wani frowned. "I heard Miss Helen telling them to get ready for the parade, but

Mr. Malkovitch said he didn't do parades."

"I thought we *all* had to do parades."

"He told Miss Helen that bears didn't take parades rightly. I don't know what that means. If elephants and horses can walk around in circles, I don't know why bears can't."

"Well, they're more dangerous, I suppose. Like tigers and lions. Oh, there's the music. Here we go!" She ran to Ruth the elephant and tapped on Ruth's knee. Ruth ran her trunk over Dixie happily.

Then Mooey Sullivan suddenly appeared. He let Dixie place her foot in his hand, and he lifted her until she was straddling the elephant's neck. "Thank you, Mr. Sullivan," she said.

"You look sharp, Dixie."

Mickey was wearing an elephant boy's costume. He always said it made him feel like an idiot, but he had to do it. Now he said, "Look at Darla. She's on stage again."

Darla was riding one of the Von Bulows' stallions. She was standing up and doing a pirouette like a ballet dancer.

"You're not on yet, Darla!" Mickey yelled. "Wait for the paying customers!" He laughed when the girl's eyes narrowed.

She yelled back, "Mind your own business!"

"But she sure is pretty. I wish I were that pretty," Dixie murmured.

"All a matter of taste," Mickey said. "You look good in that outfit. Not like this stupid thing I have to wear."

"You look good, too, Mickey. That's the way an elephant boy is supposed to look."

He was wearing a turban on his head and some sort of cloth wrapped around his middle. He had on trunks made of canvas, and he was barefoot. He held an elephant hook in his hand. He never used it, but the customers expected him to carry one. "Well, here we go!"

The circus band blared as the performers marched around the ring. Dixie sat on Ruth's neck, waving at the spectators, and they waved back. It was fun!

When the Spec was over, she changed into the white costume she wore for the bit she did with Stripes, the Siberian tiger. The act wasn't much. She just rode him around the inside of the wild animal cage. But the spectators loved seeing a small girl riding on a five-hundred-pound tiger!

As she sat on Stripes, she patted his

neck and more than once leaned forward to feed him a fried chicken liver from the small leather pouch at her waist. "That's a good tiger," she said.

Stripes would always rumble in his throat, and then she sometimes gave him another liver.

When her act was finished, Dixie watched the Flying Marinos for a while. She thrilled as Mia and Brett Bailey, Mia's partner, flew through the air to be caught by her father. Mrs. Marino was also in their act. She saw to it that the trapezes were there when the flyers returned. Dixie had been surprised to learn that just getting back to the trapeze platform was one of the hardest things a flyer had to do.

"We practice getting back up on that stand every day," Mia had told her. "It's harder than you think, and Mama has to have that trapeze at exactly the right place at exactly the right moment, or we'd fall to the net."

Dixie loved to watch the Marinos. There was something so graceful about them as they flew through the air. Sometimes they "balled up." That meant folding their legs and grabbing them, then making themselves into a small ball and turning over and over.

Dixie thought that Brett, with his blond hair and blue eyes, was the handsomest boy she had ever seen. When the flyers' act ended—they just dropped into the net—she said, "You were great, Brett."

"So were you, Dixie." He grinned at her.

The next act after the Marinos was announced by Nolan Miller, the owner and ringmaster. He was a tall and portly man with hair dyed black.

He said, "And now in the center ring, brought from Russia at tremendous expense, I give you the Malkovitch trained bears! These animals were captured in the wilds of Russia and are extremely dangerous! They weigh nearly a thousand pounds each and can take a man's arm off in one bite!"

Dixie well knew that Mr. Miller was not always telling the truth. The bears *were* large, but she doubted that they weighed a thousand pounds. She moved closer to watch, standing on the outside edge of the performing ring. She knew that no one could see her there. The spotlights were on the bears.

Mr. Malkovitch put the bears through their tricks, and they were marvelous indeed, Dixie thought. One bear was named Ivan, and the other was named Ilona. She heard Mr. Malkovitch talking to them. She guessed he was speaking in Russian, but she heard "Ivan" and "Ilona" again and again.

Both bears could stand on their hind legs and dance together—something that must have been very hard to do, Dixie decided. When they waltzed around under the spotlights, she laughed and clapped until her hands hurt.

Then they balanced balls on their noses and tossed them to one another. They were almost as good as Sidney Lo, the juggler. After that they both rode small bicycles.

Dixie loved the bears. Her favorite of all their tricks was when Ivan walked high overhead across a narrow board that was turned on its edge. It was the equivalent of being a high-wire bear walker. When the bear slid down to the ground, Dixie wanted to run over and hug him.

Then the act was over, and the Malkovitches led the bears out of the Big Top.

Dixie followed them. "Hey, David," she called. "That was a great act!"

David had helped his father in the performance. He guided Ilona while Mr. Malkovitch stayed close to Ivan.

"Does it always take both of you to do your act?"

"Yes, it does," he said. David looked sharp in a black Cossack outfit. He had on shiny black boots. The black trousers stuffed into them fluffed out over the boot tops. His shirt was white and blouselike with big puffy sleeves, and he wore a fur cap.

"Well, you were great."

She waited for him to say thank you, but he didn't. He simply shrugged and kept going. *That boy needs to read a book on good manners,* Dixie said to herself. Her feelings were hurt.

She went to change her costume.

After the afternoon parade, when the spectators had gone and the animals were all put up, Dixie went with Aunt Sarah to the cook tent. The cook, Clara Rendell, greeted them. She was a tall woman with red hair. She also had a loud voice, and sometimes she scared people with it. Dixie knew, however, that Miss Clara was one of the kindest women she had ever met.

"Hello, Miss Clara. You going to give me another cooking lesson today?"

Miss Clara smiled. She obviously liked Dixie very much. "I guess I can. You come over, and I'll teach you how to make a pineapple upside-down cake."

"Ooh, that sounds good!" Then Dixie saw the Malkovitches coming in. "Have you met the bear people yet?"

"They've been in to eat, but they don't say anything. Not very friendly, are they?"

Dixie remembered what Aunt Sarah had said. "Well, they're from Russia and haven't been here too long."

"It wouldn't hurt them to smile once in a while. They look like they've all got stomachaches."

Secretly, that's what Dixie thought, too.

She sat down at a table. Aunt Sarah and Bigg were on one side of her and Mickey on the other. Across from them was Wani Lo, who was flanked by Darla Castle and Eric Von Bulow.

Just then Eric thumped Wani on the ear.

Wani said sharply, "Don't *do* that, Eric! It's not funny!"

But Eric laughed. "You contortionists are all the same! No sense of humor!"

Mickey reached across the table and rapped Eric on the nose.

"*Ow!* What did you do *that* for?"

"You horse people are all the same." Mickey grinned. "You got no sense of humor."

Everyone laughed except Eric. He rubbed his nose, saying, "Well, that's not funny."

"No, it's not, so stop thumping people," Dixie advised him. "Now you see how it feels."

Eric began to shovel in his food. "What about those new people, the Ruskies?"

"Their name is Malkovitch," Aunt Sarah said quietly.

"I can't say a name like that."

"I think you can if you try hard enough," Sarah persisted.

"*You* probably like them, Darla," Mickey said with another grin. "They've been in the circus business for a long time, I guess."

Darla was wearing a fancy outfit, as usual. She always came to dinner in the cook tent dressed as if she were going to a fancy hotel. Today she had on a black jump-suit. The top was made of a stretchy, puckered material. The bottom had tiny white polka dots. She glanced over at the Malkovitches and said, "They're not people *I'd* care to be friends with. They're foreigners."

"I guess all your people were Indians,

then." Mickey egged Darla on. "I mean, Indians were the original Americans, so the rest of us are all foreigners, aren't we?"

Darla sniffed. "You know what I mean very well, Mickey Sullivan!"

"I know what you mean," Mickey said. "It means you're stuck up! What makes you so much better than people from Russia or anywhere else?"

"Well, look at them. They're sitting there all by themselves. Have any of you tried to make friends with them? I bet you have, Dixie."

"Yes, I did go by their trailer."

Darla smiled sweetly. "Did they welcome you in?"

"Well, no," Dixie admitted.

"You see what I mean? They don't *want* any friends."

That started a long conversation about the Malkovitches. Dixie was tired of the subject.

She happened to be looking when one of the girls who helped Miss Clara with the serving suddenly tripped and spilled a glass of iced tea. It went all over Gregori Malkovitch.

The bear trainer leaped up, wiping his shirt. He turned on the waitress and shouted at her in Russian. What he said, no one could understand—except his children—but it couldn't have been anything kind. The serving girl, Mary, was shy enough as it was, and clearly the big man frightened her.

Clara Rendell had seen the accident, too. She came running. Putting her arm around Mary, she said, "That's all right, dear. It was an accident. It could happen to anyone. You go along. I'll take care of it."

Now Mr. Malkovitch glared at Miss Clara. "Why don't you get help," he said in his thick accent, "that can do something right?"

"And why don't *you* learn some manners?" she demanded.

An uncomfortable silence fell over the cook tent. Everyone stopped eating and listened to them argue.

Clara Rendell had been around the circus for a long time, and everybody knew she could be as forceful as Gregori Malkovitch. "She was just trying to do her job. An accident happened. And you're not going to melt from a little tea on you."

"You are no lady!"

"And you are no gentleman! If you don't like the way we act over here, you

42

can go back to Russia or wherever it is you came from!"

Then Mr. Malkovitch shouted, "Your food is no good! I wouldn't feed it to the hogs!"

"Fine! Why don't you leave and go eat somewhere else?" Miss Clara fumed. Her face was flushed.

"That is what I *will* do! I shouldn't eat the kind of food you serve, anyway! Come!" He grabbed his daughter by the hand and led her out of the cook tent. David followed, his head bowed.

"There. You see what I mean?" Darla said. "They have no class at all."

Dixie felt terrible. She had been watching little Katy's face. She could tell that the child was frightened by the incident, although she didn't say a word. Dixie thought about her being dragged off by her father and wished that she could say something to make her feel better.

The next day all the boys and girls gathered for Sunday school in the Big Top before Mr. Sullivan's sermon.

Dixie whispered to Aunt Sarah, "The Malkovitches aren't here. I knew they wouldn't be."

Sarah began to teach the lesson. After a while, she quoted from an Old Testament Scripture verse: "You shall not oppress a stranger."

"That's Exodus 23:9," Aunt Sarah said. "Then, in Deuteronomy 10:18, the Bible says that God executes justice for the fatherless, the widow, and the stranger. Do any of you know what that means for us today?"

"I do," Darla popped up. She always wanted to give the answers. "You're supposed to be kind to widows, and orphans, and strangers."

"That's right, Darla. Now, you know what a widow is. And you know what an orphan is. But what does a 'stranger' mean?"

Darla shrugged. "Just somebody you don't know."

"Well, in those days a 'stranger' meant a foreigner. Someone who was not a Jew."

Dixie saw immediately where her aunt was going. She nudged Mickey with her elbow and whispered, "Boy, Darla's going to get it now!"

Darla was sitting up straighter since Aunt Sarah seemed to be talking directly to her.

"The strangers in this verse meant people from another country. Some of them went along with the Jewish people in their travels, and here God says that the Jews were to treat these people right." She waited, watching Darla's face. "So for us, Darla, this means that when someone comes from another country, we are to be very kind to them."

Darla was a smart young lady. She saw that Sarah was rebuking her for what she had said about the Malkovitches. She was also very proud, however. She said, "Well, they're nerds."

"Even if people seem to be 'nerds,' we're still to be kind to them, for they are far away from their homeland. So I want all of you to remember this verse. God is pleased when we are kind to widows and orphans—and foreigners."

After Sunday school, Dixie asked Mickey, "Do you think Darla will be any better to the Malkovitches?"

"Nah, she's gonna do what she wants to do. You know Darla!"

4

INCIDENT IN THE BIG TOP

"Aunt Sarah, I don't have anything to do."

Sarah looked up from the book she was reading. "Why don't you listen to your new DC Talk tape?"

"I just finished listening to that."

"Well, don't you have a new one by 4-Him?"

"I just played that one too."

"Then play with your Nintendo game."

"I'm tired of that."

Aunt Sarah pulled off her reading glasses and scowled. "You know, if there's one thing I can't stand, it's a child who says, 'I'm bored.'"

"Well, I *am* bored!"

"Look, you've got Barbie dolls, a Nintendo with probably twenty games, a CD player, all the books that the trailer will hold, a TV set—and you tell me you're bored! Give me a break, Dixie!"

Dixie knew that she was being unreasonable. She looked over her supply of videos. She picked up *The Lion King*. She was about to say, "I saw this with Mickey two nights ago," but knew that she had better not. Aunt Sarah was at the end of her patience. "I guess I'll go out and see if I can find Mickey."

"Good idea. You two find something to do."

Dixie felt sorry for herself. She didn't *want* to displease her aunt. Living with Aunt Sarah Logan was the next best thing to being with her parents.

She thought about her mom and dad as she walked among the trailers toward the Big Top. She wondered what it was like in Africa. *I'll be glad,* she thought, *when they find a place so I can be with them on the mission station.* The reason Dixie was with Aunt Sarah was that her parents had said life was too primitive at the place where they were serving. Just last week her father had written:

We're trying to get everything put together so you can come and be with us, Dixie. We miss you more than you can possibly imagine. Just be patient, and remember that we're serving the Lord here, and you must serve Him there. And one day we'll all serve Him together here in Africa.

Just the thought of her parents cheered Dixie.

She went down to see Stripes and spent some time rubbing the tiger's furry head and listening to him growl. Then she wandered among the other animal cages before finally stepping into the Big Top. Several acts were rehearsing. There was always something going on.

Overhead she saw the Flying Marinos practicing. *They ought to be good,* Dixie thought. *They don't do anything but practice!* This time it was just Mr. Marino and Brett. Dixie sat on her knees and watched the young man swing back and forth, and when he turned a double somersault and caught Mr. Marino's hands, she applauded loudly. He swung back to the platform where Mrs. Marino waited, and Dixie called up, "That was wonderful, Brett!"

"Thank you, Dixie!" Brett shouted. "You want to come up and try it?"

"No, thank you! I'll just watch!"

Then she saw some clowns working on a new act and ran to be with them. As usual, Bigg was in the middle of it. He was the smallest clown but was the boss of all of them.

They had constructed what looked like a building about fifteen feet high, and Bigg was up in a top window. It looked as if flames were gushing from the building, and the clowns below were trying to get a net ready for Bigg to jump in. Nothing they did worked, however, and Bigg kept screaming for them to save him. He was so funny that Dixie had to hold her sides, laughing.

She waited until the midget came down, then said, "That was so funny, Bigg. I hadn't seen that one before."

Wiping the sweat off his forehead, Bigg nodded. "It was my idea. Do you really like it?"

"Oh, yes! It's going to be a big hit!"

"Good. And by the way, I've got some good news for *you*," Bigg said, grinning broadly.

"What?"

"I'm gonna get hitched."

Dixie blinked with surprise. "You mean *married?*"

"Sure, married! What else could I mean?" Bigg said indignantly.

Dixie could not imagine Bigg's being married. "I didn't even know you were engaged."

"Well, I'm not—yet."

"But who's the lady?"

"Oh, I haven't picked her out yet," Bigg said. "A fellow can't jump into a thing like this."

"You mean you're going to be married, but you don't know who you're going to marry?"

"Oh, it won't be any problem. The ladies have always liked me."

"Well, I hope you'll let me know in time to get you a wedding present."

"Oh, yes. It'll probably be in all the papers."

"I'll be watching. So long, Bigg."

Dixie wandered around the Big Top until she came to the far ring where David Malkovitch was working with Ivan. She had learned to tell the difference between Ivan and Ilona. "Hi, David," she said. "How's it going?"

He whirled. "Keep away, Dixie. This bear's dangerous."

"Oh, he is not!" Dixie smiled at Ivan, who was on all fours and rocking back and forth. Suddenly he bared his fangs and groaned deep inside his chest. "Look, he's smiling at me."

"I tell you these bears are dangerous! Get back!"

"I'll bet they're not as dangerous as tigers. Look, I have some candy in my pocket. I'll bet he'd like it." She fished in her pocket and brought out a Hershey bar. It was a little sticky, but she broke off half of it and went closer. "Will it be all right to feed him?"

David frowned at her. "I don't know— Papa's awful particular about what they eat. You'd better not."

"Oh, a candy bar never hurt anybody!" Dixie held out the chocolate.

The bear took the candy and chewed on it with delight. Then his long red tongue came out, and he licked his lips. He thrust his head forward and moaned again.

"See, he's asking for more." Dixie gave

him the other half and watched as he ate it. "Can I pet him?"

"You're not supposed to! If he bit you, then you'd sue us."

"I would not, and he wouldn't bite me! He likes me! See?" Dixie ran her hand over the bear's forehead. Actually, she knew very well that she shouldn't do this. Aunt Sarah would have objected. But Ivan was so cute.

Suddenly Dixie felt herself being roughly pulled away.

"I told you to stay away from that bear!"

"Don't be pulling me around, David Malkovitch!"

"I'll pull you if you don't leave my bear alone!"

By now they were shouting.

Then, all of a sudden Dixie heard another voice.

"You leave Dixie alone, or I'll bust you!" Mickey yelled angrily.

"Both of you get away from here! I'm rehearsing my act!"

"I saw you push Dixie around! Why don't you try it on me?"

"All right, I will!" David gave Mickey a shove backward.

Immediately Mickey jumped at him, and the two boys fell to the sawdust, rolling around.

Dixie was not worried about the boys, but she did look nervously over at Ivan. She knew it wasn't good for this kind of thing to happen around large animals. She couldn't imagine Val Delaney or his brother, Kirk, scuffling in a cage full of tigers.

And then she saw that Ivan *was* upset. He was moaning deeper in his throat now. She went toward him, saying, "It's all right, Ivan. They're just playing."

Ivan looked at her and stuck out his tongue. She fished down in her pocket where there was a second Hershey bar. She ripped off the paper, broke it in two, and gave the bear a third of it. She continued to feed him while the two boys kept on wrestling.

Suddenly Mooey Sullivan was there.

"What in the world are you kids doing?"

And then Gregori Malkovitch appeared, his face pale with anger. He snatched up David and said furiously, "What's your son doing to my boy?"

"It wasn't Mickey's fault!" Dixie said.

"I might have known you'd take his side! All you Americans think you own the

54

world! Come along, David. Come, Ivan!"
Mr. Malkovitch took hold of Ivan's harness,
ready to lead him off. Then he looked at the
big bear's mouth. "Who's been feeding
candy to my bear?"

"I have. I'm sorry, Mr. Malkovitch, but
he liked it so much."

"You stay away from me, and from my
children, and from my bears!"

Mickey's hair was mussed, and he had
a red spot on his forehead. His father held
him by the arm and said, "What's the matter with you—fighting like a ruffian?"

"Well, he was pushing Dixie around."

"It's all right, Mr. Sullivan. David was
afraid I was going to bother the bear. It
wasn't really his fault either."

Mooey Sullivan shook his head. "Kids,"
he muttered. "Come on, Mickey. If you've
got enough energy to fight, I'll give you
something *worthwhile* to do."

When Dixie went home, she told Sarah
what had happened.

"Well, you were wrong to feed the bear.
You must know how much trouble animal
trainers have as it is—and for strangers to
be interfering, is unforgivable."

"But I was just feeding him a Hershey bar."

"Did David tell you not to do it while he was training the bear?"

"Well, yes, he tried to."

"And so you did it anyway. When David's father isn't there, *he's* in charge of Ivan. So you were wrong, Dixie."

Dixie pouted. She had come home expecting sympathy from her aunt, and now she was getting a sermon. "Well, Mr. Malkovitch didn't have to make such a big thing out of it."

Sarah shook her head. "I feel sorry for them. As I've told you, they're *strangers* here. They don't understand us, just as we don't always understand people in countries where we visit. Remember how much trouble we had in the Middle East, trying to understand their ways?"

"That's different."

"It's *not* different! And you did behave badly!"

"Well, I don't care. They don't want any friends!"

Aunt Sarah looked at Dixie sadly. "Everybody wants friends. Maybe they don't know how to make friends, and you're not being any help, Dixie."

Dixie's feelings smarted, and she got away from Aunt Sarah as quickly as she could.

Later that night when she said her prayers with her aunt, she found herself embarrassed. In her prayer she did not say a word about the incident in the Big Top. She was hoping Aunt Sarah would forget it.

Still later, however, when Dixie lay alone hugging Scarlett in the crook of her arm, she whispered, "Dear Lord, I didn't mean to be thoughtless. And I know You love Mr. Malkovitch even if he is a grouch. Please forgive me. I'll try to be better to him. I really will."

5

THE ACCIDENT

In spite of David Malkovitch's impoliteness, Dixie found herself being more and more attracted to Ivan. The massive bear became her animal favorite—next to Stripes, of course.

Every day she would find an opportunity to go by and visit the huge brown animal. Usually she took with her some sort of sweet. As soon as he saw her coming, he would begin rumbling and often would rear up on his hind legs. He made a rather frightening sight, but Dixie had discovered that actually he was a very gentle bear.

However, if Dixie made friends with Ivan, she made none among the Malkovitches. She had always prided herself on being able to make friends, too, but no matter how often she smiled or spoke to any of them, she got absolutely no friendly response. Certainly none from Katy. And none from David, evidently still upset with her over causing the fight between him and Mickey Sullivan. Mr. Malkovitch, of course, refused to even speak.

The Malkovitch family had not appeared in the dining room since his argument with Clara Rendell, and this troubled Aunt Sarah.

"I don't know what we should do about the Malkovitches, but we need to do something."

"We did do something," Dixie said. She had tried a new cookie recipe and now took one from where it lay cooling on the kitchen counter and tasted it. "These are good," she said. "I'm going to be as good a cook as you are, Aunt Sarah."

But Aunt Sarah was not through with the Malkovitches. "We've got to do something. They're so alone."

"That's what they want to be—alone. You can't make friends if people don't want to be friendly."

"I still think maybe they want to be but just don't know how." Aunt Sarah's brow was wrinkled into a frown. "I keep thinking what it'd be like if you or I were over in

Russia—in their country. We wouldn't speak their language very well, their ways would be different, and we wouldn't know how to go about responding to them, either."

"They're all stuck up! That's what they are! Why, that girl Katy—I would have been a good friend to her, but she won't even talk to me!" She put half of the cookies on a paper plate, covered them with foil, and said, "I'm going to give some of these to Bigg."

Dixie found Bigg sitting in front of his trailer in a folding beach chair. He looked up from the newspaper he was reading and grinned. "Hello, Dix," he said. "What's coming down?"

"I brought you some cookies."

"Hey, that's good news." Bigg sat up straight and put down the newspaper. He popped a whole cookie into his mouth, then rolled his eyes before shutting them. "Now, that's what a cookie ought to taste like!"

"It's got coconut and chocolate in it. I'm just experimenting. Maybe I'll put some pecans in them next time."

"Couldn't be much better than this."

Bigg took another, then said, "What are you up to—besides baking cookies, I mean?"

"Oh, I don't know. Everything's kind of quiet right now. When will the circus be moving on?"

"In two days. We're going to be headed up North this time. Be a little cooler up there, I hope. I can't stand this hot weather."

Dixie and Bigg sat talking a while, and she tried to get him to tell some circus stories. He had been with the circus most of his life, and he had a storehouse full of them. When she kept urging him, he said, "Well, have you heard about Ella Seaton?"

"No. Who is she?"

"She was a bareback rider." Bigg took another cookie. "One night Ella was riding her horse around the ring, and she was standing on his back in her beautiful white dress. Everything was going fine. Then somebody threw some flowers to her. I guess the flowers scared the horse, because he jumped to one side, and Ella went flying through the air." He stuffed another cookie into his mouth. "I thought she'd be killed, but she went and landed right in a box seat where a man was sitting. He jumped up and caught her. Saved her life, I expect."

"That's a nice story."

"Well, it gets even nicer than that. Ella and this man fell in love with each other, and they got married. He went with the circus, too. He became the ringmaster of The Greatest Show on Earth."

Dixie liked stories like that, and she pried several more out of the clown.

But finally Bigg got up, saying, "Well, I see I've finished these cookies. Bring some more someday, Dixie."

"I will, Bigg. And thanks for telling me stories."

Dixie roamed around the circus grounds until she heard the sound of laughing and shouting. On the other side of the Big Top she found Mickey, Wani, Eric, and Darla tossing a ball around. It looked as if they were playing some kind of game they had made up.

"Come on over, Dix!" Wani called out. "You can be on our side."

"All right."

Soon Dixie was hot and sweaty. All of the boys and girls were strong and healthy from working on their circus acts, and they played hard. Once Eric ran into Wani and sent her spinning through the air. She landed as lightly as an acrobat, though, and got up laughing.

Dixie was enjoying the game when, out of the corner of her eye, she saw Katy Malkovitch come out of the cook tent and walk across the open space beside them.

Katy was carrying a tray of something —it looked like drinks and something else. The little girl glanced at them, and Dixie hollered, "Come over and play, Katy!" But she turned away and continued to walk by.

What happened next caught everybody off guard. Darla threw the ball high in the air. Eric raced to catch it. Dixie saw that Katy was right in his way, and she heard him shout, "Get out of the way, kid, or I'll run over you!"

Katy, however, did not even turn around.

"Look out, Eric!" Dixie yelled.

But it was too late. Intent on catching the ball, Eric ran at full speed into Katy. The girl went rolling along the ground. The tray went spinning in the air, spilling food and cups of Coke everywhere.

Dixie ran to where Katy was lying.

The little girl was in tears. Her face was covered with dirt, and her cheek was bleeding where she had hit a rock.

An enraged cry suddenly split the air, and David Malkovitch came running as hard as he could. He got to the small concerned group gathered around Katy and shouldered Eric and Darla out of the way. Bending over, he picked up his little sister and held her in his arms. She clung to him as if she were a baby, her face buried against his chest.

Eric looked around guiltily, then said, "I yelled at her, but she was too stuck up to move."

David Malkovitch looked at Eric with disgust written on his face.

"She couldn't hear you! *She's deaf!*" Then he wheeled and walked away, carrying Katy and leaving the other youngsters to stare after him.

No one seemed able to say a word until finally Eric muttered, "It wasn't my fault. I didn't know the kid was deaf."

I didn't know either, Dixie thought, *but I should have.* She turned away, ignoring something that Darla was saying, and discovered that she was about to cry. Quickly she left the field and found a quiet place to sit down. Then she did cry!

6

"I DID A
BAD THING"

The accident with Katy troubled Dixie greatly, and she kept thinking about it. Eric, of course, had blustered, insisting it wasn't his fault. Darla had chimed in, saying, "There's no way that we could know the girl couldn't hear."

She remembered that Mickey, however, had refused to meet anyone's eyes, and Dixie knew him well enough to understand that he felt as bad about the incident as she did.

She tried to put what had happened out of her mind, but she couldn't.

At supper that night, Aunt Sarah studied her. "You're not eating anything, and it's your favorite dish."

Dixie looked down at her spaghetti and meatballs as if she had never seen them.

This was strange, because she had prepared them herself. Usually she ate spaghetti as if she were starving, but now she just shook her head and toyed with the long strips of pasta. "I guess I'm not very hungry," she muttered.

Sarah leaned back in her chair. The stereo was on in the background, softly playing one of Dixie's favorite songs by Point of Grace. Finally Sarah asked gently, "There's something wrong, isn't there, Dixie?"

Quickly Dixie looked up. Despite herself, tears came into her eyes. "I did a bad thing," she said simply, and when Aunt Sarah asked what, she related the incident. "I didn't know she couldn't hear! And I quit trying to be nice to her!" Then she wiped her eyes. "I just can't help thinking about that little girl getting hurt like that. And she's deaf, Aunt Sarah! Being deaf must be awful!"

"I'm sure it's very difficult," Sarah said, then waited for Dixie to say more.

Dixie pulled up a strand of spaghetti, wound it around her fork, but then put the fork down. "All day long I've been thinking about what it would be like not to be able to hear. I spend so much time listening to my CDs! And I think how hard it would be to watch movies without hearing the sound. Why, even going to church would be hard. You couldn't hear the music *or* the sermon."

Sarah nodded slowly. "It would be very hard," she repeated. "I don't think any of us that have hearing are grateful enough for it. To have our eyes—to be able to see, and hear, and walk around—every morning when we get up, we ought to thank God for these things!"

"But I guess we just take them for granted, don't we?"

"Most of the time we do. Sometimes we have to lose something before we really appreciate it."

Dixie said little that night. She watched a McGee and Me video, but she didn't really see it. She had seen it so many times that she had it almost memorized anyway, but she sat on the couch staring at the screen blankly while Aunt Sarah read.

At bedtime, Aunt Sarah came and knelt beside her bed, as she did every night, and they prayed together.

When Dixie prayed, she said, "Lord, forgive me for stopping being nice to Katy."

When Sarah prayed, she prayed not just for Katy but for all the Malkovitches, asking God to open their hearts to Him. Then she leaned over and kissed Dixie and said, "Don't worry about it anymore. You confessed it to the Lord, and it's all over. From now on we must both try to be kinder, for now we know there is even more of a reason to be kind. Good night, sweetheart."

"Good night, Aunt Sarah."

Dixie tucked Scarlett into the crook of her arm. She soon grew sleepy, but still she carried on her usual conversation with the Barbie doll.

"Aunt Sarah says I'm not supposed to worry, but I can't help it, Scarlett," she whispered. "I keep seeing Katy rolling in the dirt and her face bleeding. I keep thinking of how hurt David looked. He didn't say anything, but I could tell that he was."

She smoothed the doll's hair, then closed her eyes. The last thing she thought was: *Tomorrow I'm going to do something for Katy, and*—she was almost asleep—*and I'm going to do something for Mr. Malkovitch and David too.*

7

MISS CLARA
OUTDOES HERSELF

As soon as Dixie woke up the next morning, she said, "I don't want any breakfast, Aunt Sarah. I'm going over to see Miss Clara."

"I'm not very hungry myself." Sarah looked at her niece and started to say more but then seemed to decide that she had better not. "But eat a little something. It's not good to start the day without breakfast."

"Miss Clara always has something good. Maybe I'll eat at the cook tent."

Dixie was off at once to the tent that housed the circus kitchen and dining room. When she sat down at a table beside Wani Lo, who was eating her breakfast, Dixie discovered that she was hungry after all. As Wani talked energetically, Dixie ate a serving of ham, eggs, and homemade biscuits.

She even wangled a cup of hot chocolate out of Miss Clara, who was always partial to her.

Then, after the performers and workers had left, Dixie joined Miss Clara in the kitchen, where the cook was supervising her two helpers in cleaning up the cook tent.

"I've got to talk to you, Miss Clara."

Clara Rendell looked down at Dixie. The cook was kind-looking but big—and had a very loud voice when she chose to use it.

"Why, sure. What is it? You need a private corner? Come on over here where we won't be bothered."

She led the way to a small table. The side walls of the tent were lifted, and a gentle breeze was coming in. "What is it, honey?" Miss Clara asked.

"It's the Malkovitches, Miss Clara."

"Are they giving you trouble again? I think I'll take my frying pan and beat that big hairy man over the head!"

"No, no, don't do that, Miss Clara!" Dixie said quickly. She bit her lip and decided to make a full confession. "I've been all wrong about them. About Katy, anyway."

"That's the little girl."

"Yes, ma'am." She related the story of how Eric had accidentally hurt Katy. Then she said, "When David picked her up and told us she was *deaf,* I never felt so bad in my whole life!"

Dixie saw compassion leap into the cook's brown eyes.

"Why, I never dreamed of such a thing!"

"I don't guess any of us did, but that doesn't help. She was so pitiful with her face bleeding, and I could tell that David was hurt."

Miss Clara rested her elbows on the table. "I guess I was too sharp-tongued with those folks."

"I think we've all behaved pretty rotten. Aunt Sarah's always said they're foreigners and God tells us in the Bible that we're to be kind to them."

"I didn't know the Bible said that."

"Well, it does. I can show you sometime."

Miss Clara pulled a handkerchief out of her apron pocket and wiped her face. She appeared to be thinking deeply. Then she wagged her head. "I'll tell you what let's do. Let's try to make it up to those folks."

"How can we do that?"

"The only thing I can do is cook. What we'll do is make some of the most rambunctious goodies that you ever heard of. Then we'll take them over to them."

"Can I help, Miss Clara?"

"Why, I reckon as how you can!" She got up, pulled Dixie to her feet, and gave her a hug. "One of these days you're gonna be cooking for your own family, anyway, and you need to learn how to make pies and cakes. So you might as well start now."

The cook scurried around, taking down ingredients from a cabinet. "The first thing we'll make," she said, "is my specialty, almond tarts."

Dixie began helping by making the dough. She measured flour and butter into a mixing bowl and, using a pastry cutter, blended the mixture until it was crumbly. Then she cracked an egg into the bowl, added cream, and stirred the mixture to form a smooth mass.

After that was done, Dixie put the dough into the refrigerator and began to mix the filling. When the dough was chilled, she helped Miss Clara divide it into twelve pieces. With a rolling pin they rolled the pieces into thin circles and put them into a muffin pan, then filled them with the rich almond filling.

As soon as the tarts were in the oven, Dixie said, "Now I want to make something just by myself."

"All right. You can make some spiced nuts. Why, they're the best thing you ever tasted."

"Are they hard to make?"

"Laws, no!" The big cook chuckled. "They're real easy. Back when my husband was alive, when I'd done something to aggravate him, all I had to do was make him some spiced nuts, and it made all his bad temper go away."

"That's what we need." Dixie nodded energetically. "Something to make them feel better about us."

"Well, spiced nuts will do it. Here's the way you make them. I'll tell you, and you do it. No, wait a minute! I've got a recipe here somewhere."

Miss Clara rummaged through her cabinet drawers. Finally she came back with a yellowed sheet of paper. "I nigh onto forgot this, Dixie. My mama gave it to me when I was a young girl. See, that's her writing there. Be careful with it. I wouldn't want to lose it."

"Oh, I will, Miss Clara!"

"I'll get you all the ingredients, and you can do the work."

Dixie began reading from the old paper. Then she started to measure out the ingredients. She measured one cup sugar, four tablespoons of cinnamon, and one-fourth teaspoon of nutmeg into a small bowl. Then she put two egg whites into another bowl, beat them with a fork, and stirred a few pecans and almonds at a time into the egg whites. When the nuts were covered with egg white, she rolled them in the sugar and spice mixture, and then placed them on a greased cookie sheet. She continued doing this until all the nuts had been prepared in the same way. After that she baked the spiced nuts in the oven for twenty minutes. And she did it all by herself.

When the almond tarts and the spiced nuts were ready, Miss Clara said, "Well, let's get these over there while they're still nice and fresh."

"All right," Dixie said eagerly. "Let me carry the nuts, Miss Clara."

"Fine, and I'll take the almond tarts."

The sun was high in the sky now. It beat down on them, but Dixie hardly noticed. They came to the Malkovitch trailer, and Miss Clara knocked on the door.

Almost at once it opened, and there stood David, staring at them with a frown on his face.

"Is your daddy in, young fellow?"

He hesitated, then nodded. "Yes, ma'am." He turned his head and said, "Papa, Miss Clara's here."

Dixie knew a moment of fear, for she remembered the violent argument that he and Miss Clara had had in the cook tent. *What if he just tells us to get out?* she wondered.

When the bear handler came to the door, Dixie quickly said, "Mr. Malkovitch, we need to talk to you. Can we please come in?"

David's father was not a bad-looking man under his beard, Dixie thought, but he always looked so unhappy. He stood silently for a moment as if wondering what in the world they had come for. He seemed ready to slam the door shut. But finally he nodded. "Well, come inside."

He stepped back, and Dixie entered the trailer, followed by Miss Clara. As soon as they were inside, she saw Katy standing with a book in her hand. She had a Band-Aid on her face, and Dixie once again felt very bad.

"Mr. Malkovitch," Dixie began. "I want to tell you again. I'm so sorry about what happened to Katy. I hope you'll forgive me."

"It wasn't your fault," David said unexpectedly.

Dixie looked at him gratefully. "Well, I haven't been as nice to Katy as I should have been, but I'd really like to be her friend."

"I guess I'd better apologize, too," Clara Rendell said. She was holding the covered plate of tarts in front of her. She seemed to have difficulty speaking. "I want to tell you how sorry I am, Mr. Malkovitch, for yelling at you in the cook tent. That wasn't my place." She shifted her feet and then smiled as best she could. "I brought you all some almond tarts, my specialty. I hope you'll forget about that fuss I made and enjoy the tarts."

Gregori Malkovitch blinked, and then Miss Clara thrust the plate under his nose.

He took it. Then he sniffed the air. Cautiously he lifted a corner of the snowy white napkin on top and grunted. "Good! It smells very good!"

The little girl stood watching.

Dixie then went over to her and smiled. "I've brought you a gift, too," she said, pointing to herself, then to the spiced nuts, and then to Katy.

The gestures were very simple, and it was obvious that the child understood what was being said. She looked at her father, who nodded shortly, and she reached for a nut.

But Dixie put the whole plate into her hands. She waved her hand over it, signing, "They're all yours," and pointed at her.

Timidly Katy sampled a nut, and at once her eyes brightened. She smiled and took the plate over to David, who sampled them, too.

He said, "These *are* good!"

"I made them myself. Miss Clara showed me how."

David looked rather uncomfortable. He glanced at his father, then cleared his throat. "Papa, it was nice of Miss Clara and Dixie to come. As you have taught me, I will say thank you."

Gregori Malkovitch watched as his son bowed stiffly and said, "Thank you very much."

Then the big man appeared to be embarrassed. "Very good," he muttered. "We like tea. Some is made. Would you some have?"

Dixie drew a sigh of relief. Mr. Malkovitch was not smiling, but at least he had invited them for tea!

It was a rather strange tea party. They sat at the trailer table. David produced cups for the visitors and soon had poured them full. "It's very strong," he said. "Americans don't usually like it this way."

Dixie, as a matter of fact, didn't like it at all, but she didn't let that show. "I can tell it's very good tea," she said and smiled.

Miss Clara sipped hers. Then she said, "Why, I never tasted such good tea. Where did you get it, Mr. Malkovitch?"

"From Russia." He cautiously bit into one of the tarts and again said, "Good." He still did not smile, though. It was as if he had forgotten how. Then he tried one of the nuts, and his eyes, too, opened with surprise. "Very good." He nodded again.

The tea party was brief. Miss Clara complimented Gregori Malkovitch and the children on how nice and neat their trailer was, and after that there seemed to be nothing left to say.

"Well, I guess we'd better be going," Dixie said. "Thank you for the tea."

Mr. Malkovitch rose, followed by David and even Katy. David and his father bowed stiffly, and, seeing this, Katy made a small curtsy.

When Dixie and the cook were out of hearing distance, Dixie said, "Well, that went all right."

"Did you think so? I didn't."

Dixie stared up at her. "What do you mean? He didn't throw us out."

"No, he didn't, but he didn't say thank you, either. Did you notice that?"

"I guess I didn't. I was too scared to notice a thing like that."

Miss Clara took big strides as they crossed the circus grounds. A frown was on her face. But when they got to the cook tent, she said, "You know what, Dixie?"

"No. What?"

"I'm going to make that man smile!"

Dixie looked into the big woman's face, then giggled. "I think you'll have to take your fingers and turn his mouth up. I don't think he knows how to smile."

"I think he does. But we'll see. I'm gonna make him smile and say thank you, or my name's not Clara Rendell!"

Miss Clara was as good as her word. She tried. The next day she and Dixie made another trip to the Malkovitch trailer. This time they were bearing fresh biscuits and homemade blackberry jam.

Mr. Malkovitch let them in, stared at them, and took the items but seemed not to know what else to do.

Dixie was embarrassed by his silence, as was David, apparently.

Then, on the trailer wall, she happened to notice the picture of a very lovely woman in an old-fashioned picture frame. It was a black and white picture. Dixie said, "Was that your wife? She's very pretty."

Instantly Gregori Malkovitch grew angry. "That was my wife! She died—God robbed me!"

Dixie was shocked by his angry response.

When she and Miss Clara left, David followed them outside. "I'm sorry about my papa. He misses Mama so much."

"I bet you do, too, David," Dixie said.

David lowered his head and stared at the ground. *"Da,"* he said, "but Papa, he blames God."

"That's wrong," Dixie said.

"My papa doesn't think so." David turned and walked back to the trailer with his shoulders bent and his head down.

Miss Clara and Dixie said nothing until he had closed the door. Then the cook said, "It's going to be harder to make Gregori Malkovitch smile than I thought."

"You can do it, Miss Clara," Dixie said. "Any woman that can make almond tarts like you do can do most anything!"

8
DIXIE AND KATY

Dixie was sitting on the couch when Aunt Sarah came into the trailer. Her legs were crossed beneath her. The TV was off.

Aunt Sarah put down the groceries, saying, "And what are you doing?"

"Oh, nothing. Just sitting here."

Sarah laughed. "You never just sit!" she said, beginning to unload the sacks. She put the milk in the refrigerator, along with the butter and eggs, then started on the nonperishable items. "Are you up to something?"

Dixie was indignant. "You mean, am I thinking about something that will get me in trouble?"

"Well, you have been known to do such things."

"No, I'm not! I'm just thinking about Katy Malkovitch."

Sarah had a loaf of bread in her hand, and she paused before putting it in the shelf. "You've been thinking about her a lot the last few days."

"I've been doing more than thinking," Dixie said. "I've been asking God to tell me what to do."

"Well, has He told you anything?"

"I think so."

"Can you share it with me?"

"I still remember the sign language I learned when we had Dolly. I think it would be good if I taught Katy how to sign."

"Why, that's a wonderful idea! Do you think Mr. Malkovitch will let you do it?"

"I don't know. I don't see why he wouldn't."

"I don't either. That poor child must be very lonely. I wonder how she gets along even with her father and her brother. I suspect they know each other so well that somehow they just understand what each wants."

Dixie jumped up. "I'm going over and start right now." She ran back through the trailer to the small bookcase over her bed.

When she found the book she wanted, she bolted out of the trailer, slamming the door behind her.

"I told you not to slam the door!" Aunt Sarah called after her, but it was too late.

Sarah Logan stood at the trailer door for a moment, thinking about Dixie. At times she worried that she was not capable of being both father and mother to the girl, but she also had the strong feeling that God had put Dixie in her charge, at least for a time. So she sat down at the table, bowed her head, and began to pray that she would always have wisdom. She prayed, also, that Dixie would find favor with Gregori Malkovitch.

Dixie went first into the Big Top, where Mr. Malkovitch and his son were working on their act. Both Ivan and Ilona were riding bicycles today, a sight that always delighted her. To see the huge animals on the small, specially made bicycles was funny and at the same time amazing. She did not see Katy.

Then Dixie saw her too. The little girl had climbed to the very top row in the portable stands. Presumably, she had been watching the bears practice from up there. When Dixie started to climb the bleachers to sit beside her, Katy watched her come. However, she did not smile.

Dixie did smile, and she signed, "Hello, Katy." She suspected that, even without being taught, Katy knew what she was getting at. But she had determined to start from the very beginning.

She sat down beside Katy and opened the book. It was a picture book of animals. She turned to the picture of a bear, pointed at it, and then signed the letters for bear.

"See. This spells bear. B—E—A—R."

Katy watched her.

The word *bear* was written in large print underneath the picture. Dixie pointed at the B, then made the sign for B. She did the same for the other letters and spelled it all again. "Bear," she said, putting a finger on the picture. She pointed at Katy and then at Katy's hand. "You do this." She made the B sign once more.

Katy caught on at once. She made the sign for B, and then, when Dixie made the sign for E, she duplicated that. When she had spelled out all the letters with Dixie, she spelled out the word by herself. "B—E—A—R." Then she pointed to the picture of the bear.

Dixie gave the little girl a hug. "That's wonderful! Now, I'm going to teach you the alphabet." At first she had trouble getting this across, but she quickly discovered that the little girl was very bright. She taught Katy almost half the alphabet, and then she went back to the animal pictures and signed each word.

Finally, she pulled out a diagram that she had slipped in the book, and Katy's eyes grew wide. It was the picture of a hand signing the different letters. Katy studied the picture. Then she put her hand on the A and signed, "A." Next, she went to the B.

"That's exactly right! You're doing so well!" Dixie exclaimed. "Go on! Go on and do the rest of them."

For the first time, Dixie saw a smile on Katy Malkovitch's face. She was enjoying herself, and Dixie was very pleased. "You're so smart," she said. "You'll be signing in no time."

"What are you doing up here?"

Dixie started, then turned to see that David had climbed the stands. She had not

heard him coming, and she was embarrassed.

"I'm just teaching Katy how to sign."

David stared at her. "What do you
mean, *sign?* What is that?"

"Why, it's a way that you can talk with
your hands. Haven't you ever seen anybody
sign?"

David frowned. "I don't think so."

Dixie pointed at the chart. "Look. You
hold your hand a different way for each let-
ter of the alphabet. See?" She touched the
bear picture and Katy's hand. "Spell bear,
Katy."

Proudly Katy spelled out bear by signing and then beamed at David.

David gave Dixie a doubtful look. "It
would be too slow to spell out everything."

"Oh, you don't spell everything out
with letters. You only spell things that
there's not a sign for."

"I don't understand."

"Well, for example, the word *father*."
She made the number *five* with her hands
and touched her forehead once.

As he stood puzzling over this, Dixie said,
"You know, if you and your father could
learn how to sign, you could talk to Katy."

David shook his head sadly. "Papa doesn't like new things, and I don't have time for games."

Suddenly, from the arena below, David's name was called. He looked down to where his father was motioning him to come back to help with the bears. "I have to go," he said. "No, I don't think Papa would like this. He doesn't like new things."

Dixie watched as David went back down the stands. Then she turned Katy, who was watching her expectantly. *I don't know what I should do,* she thought. *It wouldn't be right to hide things from Mr. Malkovitch—but Katy's so lonely.*

Dixie had deceived her aunt once. She had arranged with Bigg to put a kitten in a certain place so that she could say she *found* it. She had learned a hard lesson. *No, she thought, I can't do that again. I'll talk to Mr. Malkovitch. Surely he won't mind someone trying to help his daughter.*

Then she felt a tug on her sleeve.

Katy was pointing down to where Helen Langley's dog, Tater, was trotting across the arena. She glanced at the signing chart and signed, "D—O—G." Then she looked at Dixie to see what she would do.

Dixie hugged the girl again and quickly signed to her, "That's good." And then she signed, "I love you, Katy," by pointing to herself, crossing her arms over her chest, and then pointing at Katy.

Tears came into Katy's eyes, and Dixie saw that she understood what that signing meant.

Now Katy Malkovitch made *her* statement. She pointed at herself, crossed her small arms over her small chest, and then she pointed at Dixie.

Dixie knew that she had done something good, and the guilty feeling that she'd had for mistreating the girl was all gone.

"You're going to be signing like everything," she whispered. "Now, let's spell some more."

9
BIRTHDAY PARTY

One of the bears has some sort of a problem, Dixie. I've got to go see about it. Would you like to come along?"

Dixie looked up from her Nintendo game and nodded eagerly. "Yes! Let me get my sandals on."

She was wearing a new outfit that she had just bought at the Gap—khaki shorts, a sky blue shirt that buttoned down the front and had two large pockets, and now a pair of brown sandals. As soon as she was ready, they walked over to the cages where the bears were kept.

Gregori Malkovitch was waiting for them. "Ah, Dr. Logan," he said and bowed. "I am glad you have come."

"I just heard that one of your bears is having problems."

"It is Ilona here. She is not eating, and she moves her head in a strange way."

Ilona was sitting down. She eyed the doctor as Aunt Sarah approached.

"Could you make her open her mouth, Mr. Malkovitch?"

"Yes. That I can do." He bent over and whispered softly to the huge bear and touched her muzzle.

At once the bear opened her mouth, and quickly Sarah leaned forward with a flashlight and looked inside. Right away she stepped back. "She's got a tooth broken off, Mr. Malkovitch."

"A tooth broken off? How could that happen?"

"I couldn't say, but I'm afraid it will have to come out."

Gregori Malkovitch shook his head sadly. "In all my life, I have never heard of such a thing except once. At one of the circuses back in Russia, a bear had a bad tooth. This was many years ago. They could never get the bear to let anyone touch him."

Sarah was silent for a moment. "I think we will have to give her a general."

Gregori blinked. "A general? You mean like in the army?"

"No." She smiled. "I mean a general anesthetic. That means we will have to put her to sleep."

"You can do this yourself?"

"Oh, yes. It won't be too difficult. I've never pulled a tooth for a bear before, though. Perhaps you'd rather get someone else."

"No. You do it. What do we do first?"

"I will have to go get some special equipment," Sarah said. "We can do it as soon as I have gone into town and bought some drugs."

After her aunt left, Dixie stayed with the bears for a while. Aunt Sarah had warned her, "Just don't get close to Ilona today. She's not feeling well, and she may be grouchy."

So Dixie sat down outside Ivan's cage and watched him. She had not brought him anything to eat today, so after a while she went over to the cook tent to beg some chopped beef from Miss Clara. While there, Dixie told the big cook about the sick bear.

"I hope the poor thing's all right soon," Miss Clara said.

"Mr. Malkovitch is really worried," Dixie said.

"I guess he might be. He makes all his living from those bears. You tell him that I'll be praying about his sick bear."

"All right, Miss Clara. And thanks for the beef."

Dixie returned to the bears and their trainer. "Could I give Ivan some of this beef?" she asked Mr. Malkovitch. "Miss Clara sent it over."

The man looked at the chopped beef and nodded gloomily. "I guess that would be all right."

"And Miss Clara said she's praying about your sick bear."

Surprise washed across the Russian's face. He stroked his beard in confusion and then asked, "She said that?"

"Yes, and I will, too."

The bear trainer gave Dixie a long look, but he said nothing more.

And then Aunt Sarah returned.

Dixie never forgot the operation, for that was what it was. Aunt Sarah had Mr. Malkovitch feed Ilona some pills. The bear became very sleepy and lay down, and then Aunt Sarah gave her a shot. Soon she was sleeping soundly, all sprawled out.

"Now I think we can do it. She's completely out," Sarah said.

Mr. Malkovitch hovered over her as she opened the bear's mouth and reached in with a pair of what looked like stainless steel pliers. "I hope I'm strong enough to do this," she said. But she gave a tug, and suddenly the tooth was out!

"Now," she said, "let me put some disinfectant on that." She sprayed the bear's mouth, put in cotton pads, and stayed beside Ilona until the bleeding had stopped.

"There. She ought to be fine when she wakes up."

"I thank you very much. Very much."

Katy had been watching, and now Dixie walked over to her and signed, "Hello," one of the words Katy had learned.

Immediately the girl signed back. Then she signed something else, and Dixie said out loud, "Well, I didn't know that!"

"What is that she's saying?" David said, coming up just then.

"She says it's her birthday."

"It is. She's seven years old today."

"Is she having a party?"

David glanced toward his father—he

was still hovering over Ilona—and shook his head, saying nothing.

"Not having a party!" Dixie cried. She turned to her aunt, who was preparing to leave. "Why, Aunt Sarah, we can have a party for her, can't we?"

"Of course. It's a little late, but we can do something. All of you come over to our trailer after the performance this afternoon, then. We'll make cake and have ice cream."

"No, no, it would be an imposition," Mr. Malkovitch protested.

"Oh, that's nonsense. We'd love to do it." Dixie's aunt smiled, and Aunt Sarah had a very winning smile.

Dixie quickly signed "birthday party" to Katy.

The little girl's eyes shone, and Dixie saw that she had understood.

Mr. Malkovitch glanced at Katy and looked ready to say no.

"See, Mr. Malkovitch, you can tell that she really wants to come."

Again clawing at his heavy beard, Gregori Malkovitch said, "Well, just this once."

Clara Rendell had not only come to the birthday party, but she had also brought an enormous cake. She said, "It's chocolate. I never heard of a chocolate birthday cake, but it's my secret recipe."

Then she beamed at Mr. Malkovitch, who was backed up in a corner, for the trailer was full. David and Katy and Dixie were there, of course, but Mickey Sullivan, Wani Lo, Eric and Marlene Von Bulow, and even Darla Castle had come, too.

"Here, put the cake right up on the counter. We've got to have candles though for Katy to blow out." Miss Clara hunted around in her pocket. "Here. I had some candles left over from your last birthday party, Dixie. Why don't you put them in and light them, and then Katy can blow them out."

Dixie put seven candles into the cake frosting and opened a matchbox. She handed one to Katy. "You light them, Katy," she signed.

Katy at once caught on. She struck the match and lit her seven candles.

Dixie took the match, and blew it out, then signed to her, "Make a wish."

Katy looked confused, and Dixie repeated her command.

Then Katy smiled brilliantly and blew out all the candles.

"Now, you'll get what you wished for!" Dixie smiled.

"What did she wish for?" Katy's father asked.

"I don't know. Why don't you ask her?"

Gregori looked embarrassed. "Well, we can't really ask things like that."

"Well, I can," Dixie said, and she asked the question, using the sign language.

At once Katy's hands moved.

"What did she say?" Gregori Malkovitch asked, seemingly fascinated at the exchange.

"She said she wishes she could talk to her papa and her brother."

Mr. Malkovitch looked down at the floor and said nothing for a while.

The silence was embarrassing, and Sarah said quickly, "Dixie, cut the cake while I get out the ice cream."

Soon everyone was busy eating cake and ice cream.

Katy seemed bashful, but David leaned toward Dixie and whispered into her ear, "I've never seen my sister so happy."

"She's such a sweet girl. So pretty too."

"Yes, she is."

After the cake was eaten, Dixie said, "We have some presents for Katy. Just little things, because there wasn't time."

Big-eyed, Katy stared at the gifts as they were placed in her hands, and when she understood that they were hers, she looked at her father. She signed, "Is it all right?" and Dixie interpreted.

"Yes, is all right," Mr. Malkovitch said.

He watched as Katy opened the gifts. None of them was expensive, but he obviously saw how much she enjoyed them. His eyes met David's, and he murmured, "We should have done this ourselves."

"Yes, we should have, Papa."

After the presents were opened, Dixie gathered the boys and girls. "Come on. Now we'll go back, and I'll show you my new Barbie doll."

"Have you got another doll?" Eric groaned. "You must have a million of them!"

The adults stayed in the living room to watch a video on the history of the circus. Everybody else went with Dixie to the rear of the trailer. It was crowded, and they had to stand in the aisle that went down through the middle of the trailer, but Dixie proudly pulled out her Barbies.

Darla, of course, sniffed. "When are you going to outgrow dolls, Dixie?"

"Never!" Dixie said firmly. "I collect them."

Katy had never seen Dixie's Barbies, and the little girl's eyes were bright as she looked at every doll.

Finally Dixie signed, "One of them is my present to you for your birthday, Katy."

"For me?"

"Yes. You can have any one you want."

Katy looked over the doll collection and immediately picked up Scarlett.

Dixie's heart sank. Her favorite doll. She hesitated, for she had meant to add, "Except Scarlett," but she had forgotten. Now her eyes met Mickey's, and she saw that he understood at once what her problem was. Dixie swallowed hard and bravely said, "Well, you picked a good one, Katy. I hope you like her."

For some time, as the group stood there, Dixie struggled with sadness at losing Scarlett. But when she saw how Katy clung to the Barbie and looked at her with shining eyes, she knew that she had done the right thing.

"I'll get you another Scarlett doll," Mickey whispered, leaning close.

"No, it wouldn't be the same. But thank you."

"You're a pretty keen kid, Dixie. Not many girls would give up their favorite doll."

It was shortly after this that things went bad. Mr. Malkovitch had gotten up to get a drink of water, and, unfortunately, he heard Darla—who had to say something bad about everyone—say, "I'm tired of fooling with that deaf kid! She's nothing but a pest!"

Dixie was horrified, and so was Mickey.

And suddenly Mr. Malkovitch was there, looming over them. He took Katy's arm, saying, "We go home. You come, David."

He stormed out of the trailer, pulling Katy along with him. David, looking stunned, followed.

Dixie was almost in tears. "You see what you did, Darla?"

"Well, I didn't mean for him to *hear* it."

"It was a rotten thing to say even if he didn't hear it!" Mickey said.

Aunt Sarah and Miss Clara both came back to find out what the trouble was.

When they found out, both shook their heads in grave displeasure. Dixie's aunt said, "You shouldn't have said such a thing, Darla."

Darla, who was not accustomed to being rebuked, stuck her nose in the air and said, "I don't have to listen to this!" And she walked down the aisle and out of the trailer.

And then Dixie glanced at the Barbie dolls on her bed. "Look," she said. "Katy left Scarlett."

"What do you mean?" Aunt Sarah asked.

"Dixie said she could have any doll she wanted, and Katy chose Scarlett," Mickey explained.

Aunt Sarah said, "Well, I declare! I know that was your favorite, Dixie."

"I'll have to take it back to her. Can I do it now, Aunt Sarah?"

"Perhaps you'd better wait until tomorrow. Mr. Malkovitch is very angry right now, and I don't blame him too much. If someone made a remark about you, I'd get mad, too."

"But I'd just go to the door and give it to her. Please, Aunt Sarah."

"Well, all right, but hurry back."

Dixie almost ran across the lot. It was dark, but there were always floodlights burning to illuminate the spot where the trailers were parked. When she knocked at the Malkovitches' trailer, David opened it almost at once.

"I brought Scarlett for Katy," she said, holding out the doll.

David shook his head. "Papa won't let her have it. He's very upset."

"I'm so sorry. I wish it hadn't happened. But really, Scarlett belongs to Katy. I gave it to her."

David stepped outside and closed the door. He looked sad. "My papa is very sad about my mama, and so am I. We miss her so much, but Katy is the saddest of all. And she is so cut off from people because she is deaf." He hesitated, then said, "Will you teach me how to sign, Dixie?"

Dixie was delighted. "Sure! It won't be hard. You're so smart, David."

"It'll have to be a secret, though," David warned. "Papa wouldn't like it."

"Well, we just won't tell him."

David said, "I don't like keeping secrets from Papa."

"I know what you mean," Dixie said. "I kept one from Aunt Sarah and did something that she wouldn't have liked. It wasn't any fun at all."

"My papa's a good man," David said defensively. "He just misses Mama so much, and he blames God for taking her away."

"He mustn't do that."

"I know, but I did the same thing for a while. We were all so lonely. You should have seen her, Dixie. She was so pretty and so much fun."

"I know it must be very hard, and extrahard for Katy. But once you can *talk* to her, think of all the things you can do together."

David bowed his head. "One day," he said softly, "God will make my papa's heart to soften. Then he can learn to talk to Katy, too. You'll help, won't you, Dixie?"

Dixie reached out and took his hand, and squeezed it. "Yes, I will. You and I, we'll pray for him, and one day all three of you will be talking together."

So why did Dixie have this uncomfortable feeling that she shouldn't be keeping secrets from Mr. Malkovitch?

10

WOMAN ON THE WARPATH

What are you doing all these afternoons you're out, Dixie?" Aunt Sarah asked idly. The two had just finished the afternoon performance, had come home to shower, and now were working on supper, which would be Dixie's favorite—spaghetti and meatballs.

Dixie watched the water boil and carefully put the dry spaghetti into it. She liked to see the pasta collapse from stiff sticks into wiggly forms that looked somewhat like worms. "Oh, nothing," she said.

"I hope you're not doing something naughty."

"Oh, no. I promise you I'm not. For one thing, David is teaching me a lot about training Ivan. Why, Ivan will obey my commands just as quick as he will David's now."

Aunt Sarah was making the salad, but at that she stopped and looked up with concern in her face. "Sometimes I worry about you being around those big bears. They're dangerous."

"Oh, fuzz!" Dixie sniffed. "Ivan's as gentle as a kitten." But she knew Aunt Sarah worried that she was not careful enough around the large animals.

"I don't suppose Mr. Malkovitch has allowed Katy to play with the doll you gave her."

"No, and she wants it so bad, but he says no."

They finished the meal preparations and sat down. After the blessing, Dixie cut off a piece of the French bread they had browned in the oven, and she smeared it with yellow butter.

Aunt Sarah liked to put Tabasco sauce over her spaghetti, and as she did so, Dixie said, "That looks just awful! You're ruining your spaghetti!"

"You eat it like you want it. I'll eat it like I want it," Aunt Sarah said happily.

"It looks like it would burn your tongue off."

Dixie shuddered, but she was accustomed to Aunt Sarah's tastes in Chinese and Mexican food. She ate her own spaghetti, and then they had chocolate ice cream for dessert.

"You want to lie down and take a nap before the evening performance?"

"No, I think I'll just walk around awhile. Maybe I'll go over and see Mickey."

"All right. But don't be late."

Dixie did go by to see Mickey, but he was playing ball with his father. Mickey wanted to be a big league baseball player someday, and Mr. Sullivan, who had played in the minor leagues himself, was teaching him how to pitch.

Dixie watched for a while, then wandered away. Eventually she went to see Ivan and found David by the bears' cages.

"Hello, David," she said. "Is Ilona all right?"

"Yes. She is fine. No problem at all. I wish I had Miss Sarah for a dentist. When I had to have a tooth pulled, it hurt like everything. That was in Russia. The dentist didn't even use any anesthetic. We were way back in the country, though."

"How about if we study some more signing?"

David's eyes lit up. "Oh, yes! Come. Over there."

They sat down behind Ivan's cage.

"Are you practicing signing every day?" Dixie asked.

"Yes, and Katy loves it. We are learning together. She is much quicker than I am, I'm afraid."

"All right, now. Here's the lesson for today. I'm going to teach you the special sign for each circus animal."

Dixie and David were so busy with their lesson that neither of them heard Mr. Malkovitch coming, but it was soon clear that he heard them. He walked to where they were behind the cage and looked down. At once his face turned red.

"David, what are you doing?"

"Papa—"

"Never mind! I see what you're doing! Didn't I tell you not to have anything more to do with this?"

"But, Papa, it would be good for Katy."

"I will decide that! I am the father, not you!" Then he turned on Dixie. His voice shook as he said, "I forbid you to teach this thing to my son or to my daughter! I will take care of my family! You will keep your nose out of it."

Dixie had never been talked to as Gregori Malkovitch spoke to her. When he wheeled and walked away, she found that she was trembling.

Quickly she left the tent where the animals were kept and walked almost blindly around the circus grounds. It was all she could do to keep from crying, and she kept her head down so that no one would see her face.

For that reason she suddenly ran right into someone. Then she felt two strong arms go around her.

"You'd better watch where you're going! You're liable to walk into the path of a car!"

Dixie looked up and saw that it was Clara Rendell. "I–I'm sorry." she whispered.

Miss Clara leaned over and looked closely at her. "What's wrong? You're crying!"

"No, I'm not!"

"Well, then, you're about to." The big cook put an arm across Dixie's shoulder and said, "You come to my trailer."

And Dixie allowed herself to be led to Miss Clara's place.

As soon as they were inside, Miss Clara sat her down and began to ask questions.

Dixie did not want to say anything about Mr. Malkovitch, but Clara Rendell was a forceful woman, and finally she came out with the whole story. "I was just trying to help, and he was so mean to me!" The tears did come then.

The kindly cook held Dixie tightly, patting her back and smoothing her hair.

Finally, when Dixie had stopped crying, Miss Clara said, "Now, you go wash your face. We have a visit to make."

"Where are we going, Miss Clara?"

"You will see."

Dixie washed her face, and then they left the cook's trailer. Clara Rendell walked with big steps, and Dixie almost had to run to keep up with her. Miss Clara was such a big woman. And for some reason, Miss Clara's face was red.

"We're not going to talk to Mr. Malkovitch, are we?"

"Yes, we are!"

"We'd better not, Miss Clara! He's awful mad at me already."

"You let me worry about that."

Miss Clara led Dixie straight up to the

Malkovitches' trailer. She knocked loudly on the door with more force than necessary.

The door opened, and when Gregori Malkovitch appeared, Clara Rendell simply mounted the two steps and pushed her way in. Dixie, not knowing what else to do, followed her.

"I'm gonna have a little talk with you, Gregori Malkovitch," the cook said, facing the big man.

"You were not invited here!"

"I invited myself! Now, you stand right there. Or sit down. Or lie down! It doesn't make any difference to me!" Miss Clara was using her loud voice.

Dixie saw David looking at the cook with wide eyes. She guessed that he had never before seen his father talked to like this. David pulled Katy inside the circle of his arm, and the two stared in disbelief at the drama before them. Dixie went to stand on the other side of Katy, and none of them said a word.

"You get out of my home at once!" Mr. Malkovitch ordered. His face was flushed—at least the part that showed above his beard.

"I'll get out when I've said what I have to say!"

The Russian seemed truly stunned. Perhaps, for once, he did not know how to handle a situation. He was a strong man and was accustomed to being obeyed, but this tall woman with the flashing brown eyes—well, he hardly knew what to do about her!

Finally he muttered, "Well, say it and then get out!"

"You are a rotten father!" the cook said. "You have two beautiful children, and you don't even want to help them!"

"That is not true! I want the very best for my children!"

"Then you take a funny way of showing it!" Miss Clara shot back. "I know Dixie gave Katy a doll—"

"*I* will buy any dolls for my daughter!"

"Have you bought her one?" she demanded.

Mr. Malkovitch's eyes shifted to Katy, but he did not speak.

"Well, have you?" Miss Clara demanded again.

"That is not your business!"

"Everyone in this circus has tried to be

a friend to you, Gregori Malkovitch. They have tried to be good to your son and your daughter, but what have you done? You've shut yourself in this trailer and bitten the head off anybody that's tried to be kind! Why, you're like an angry old bear that bites everybody that comes in sight!"

"That–is–not–so!" Gregori's voice was not as steady now, and he swallowed hard. His eyes went to the picture of his wife, and he cleared his throat. "You do not understand! You do not know what it is like! I had a good wife, and God took her . . ."

Clara Rendell stepped closer. Her face was less than a foot away from the big man's. "I loved my husband as much as you loved your wife. When he died, though, I didn't crawl into a hole and shut out the world! I didn't shut out love and treat people as you do. What's wrong with you, anyway?"

Dixie saw that Gregori Malkovitch could not answer. From where she stood, she also could see that the big man was trembling. And as Miss Clara continued to talk to him very straightforwardly, Dixie thought with surprise, *Why, he's scared, and he looks like he's about to cry!*

Then Clara Rendell must have seen the same thing, for her voice grew quiet as she said, "I'm sorry about your wife. It's always hard to lose someone we love. But do you know what, Gregori?"

The man's eyes blinked when she called him by his first name as if he were a friend.

"If I know where something is, it isn't lost, is it?"

Mr. Malkovitch looked astonished. "No, of course not."

"Well, I know where my husband is. He is with Jesus. So if I know where he is, he isn't lost. Was your wife a godly woman?"

"I know she trusted in Jesus."

"Then she is with the Savior, and she's not lost."

The room grew very still.

Then Miss Clara turned to Dixie and said, "Come along, Dixie."

Dixie gave Katy a quick squeeze before she started to leave.

When they got to the door, Clara Rendell looked back and said, "There are people who would love you, but you've become such an unkind man—even to your own children—that you make it very hard." She turned and left.

As soon as the door closed, the Malkovitch trailer was completely silent for a long time. Finally Mr. Malkovitch turned to his son and said in a strained voice, "Am I like that—like that woman says?"

David Malkovitch had always loved his father, and he still did. But now he stood straighter as he tightened his grip around his sister. "A little bit, Papa."

Gregori Malkovitch turned and walked down the narrow corridor that led through the trailer.

David heard the bedroom door shut quietly, and then he looked down at his sister. Signing, she was asking him what was happening.

"Papa just learned something about himself, I think," he said gently.

11

A NEW FAMILY

Sunday school was over, and Dixie was sitting high up in the stands, waiting for church to start. She was talking to Mickey Sullivan on her left and Wani Lo on her right. All of a sudden she stiffened, and her eyes opened wide.

"Look!" she said in amazement. "Look who's come to church!"

Her two companions followed the direction of her gesture, and it was Mickey who gasped, "Why, it's that old sourpuss Gregori Malkovitch!"

Wani Lo grasped Dixie's arm. "I never thought I'd see *him* come to church. I thought he said he would never come."

"I think the reason is right beside him," Dixie said and smiled broadly.

"And that's Miss Clara. Are they coming to church *together*?"

"I think they are," Dixie said, smiling more broadly than ever. "She vowed she would make him be polite to her, and it looks like she's done more than that." Dixie stood up on the grandstand, waved wildly, and shouted, "Hey, Clara!"

Clara Rendell was holding Katy's hand. Gregori Malkovitch was walking beside her. David was on his left. Miss Clara grinned back at Dixie. Then she said something to the big man, and the four of them started climbing the stands.

When they got close to Dixie and her friends, Clara said, "How about these seats, Gregori? In front of the children."

"I—I suppose they're fine." The Russian glanced around and looked bewildered. "This place is not like our churches in Russia."

"Well, you're not in Russia now. And it's not like our churches in America, either." Clara smiled. "But you're going to like it."

Dixie got up and said, "Here, Katy. You sit here," signing and then pointing.

Katy sat and looked about her with something like fear in her eyes.

126

David looked nervous, too. He was wearing a new blue suit with a white shirt and a tie, exactly like the one his father wore.

They looked overdressed for church in a circus, and Dixie made up her mind right then. *I'm going to educate them that they can come to this church wearing anything.* Aloud, she said, "I'm going to sit where I can sign the sermon for Katy."

She moved down to the bleacher below Katy and turned around to face her. As soon as the singing started—led by Russell Hamilton Bigg himself—she began to sign the words to the song, singing them at the same time.

It was easy to see that all of this was totally new to the Malkovitches. They had no doubt been in large, formal churches in Russia, and it was clear that they hardly knew what to think of all this. Down below were the rings where they performed everyday. Down below was Mooey Sullivan, who, when he was not preaching, was leading his troupe of elephants in their act. In front of Mooey sat his wife, Irene, playing on a portable organ.

Dixie sang and made the signs for "The Old Rugged Cross."

She saw that Miss Clara had brought along one of the church's tattered, paper-back songbooks. She put it in front of Mr. Malkovitch at the right page. He looked embarrassed, but Miss Clara just sang very loudly. On the second verse, he began to sing a little. And Clara said, "What a beautiful, strong voice you have, Gregori!"

The Russian still looked embarrassed, but David was proud. He leaned down to Dixie and said, "My papa was always a good singer."

"Well, sing out," Clara said. "We need lots of good singers in this church."

Katy kept watching Dixie and seemed able to follow along sometimes. Dixie thought, *I've got to learn to sign better. There's so much I don't know.* When she got to a word that she could not possibly sign with a gesture, she did the best she could. In that case, she would always think quickly and sign a word close to the one she didn't know.

Finally the singing was over, and Rev. Mooey Sullivan, elephant handler, stood up and began to preach.

"My text this morning is from the gospel of John. It is from the words of the Lord Jesus, 'You must be born again.'"

Dixie tried hard to keep up, but she

knew that she was missing a lot of Mooey's sermon. She did not know how to make a sign for "born," and she resolved that she would find a way to sign it before the next church service. However, she did her best, and she was rewarded by seeing Katy following some of it with a happy expression in her eyes.

Halfway through Mooey Sullivan's message, Mr. Malkovitch, who had been listening intently, murmured to Miss Clara, "What does it mean born again? I do not understand this."

She turned in surprise. "You don't know? But you went to church in Russia . . ."

"Yes, but this born again I do not know. I was baptized when I was a baby and later went to church when I could. But it is not easy in the circus."

Clara Rendell reached over and patted his arm. "You and I will talk more about this."

"Very well. Are you . . . 'born again'?"

"Yes, indeed." She smiled. And when Clara Rendell smiled, she was a handsome woman indeed.

Dixie saw and heard all of this, and she winked up at Aunt Sarah, who was sitting behind the Malkovitches.

Sarah gave her the "V for victory" sign and smiled back brightly.

"Well, my papa is so happy about you helping Katy."

David Malkovitch was standing beside Ivan, getting ready to put him on his bicycle. Ivan did not particularly like the bicycle, but he was obedient. When he was seated on it, David gave him a little push, and the bear went around and around inside the circle.

David then tried to get Ilona on her bicycle. But she liked the bicycle even less than Ivan did, and finally David gave up. "I cannot do both. I'll have to wait for Papa." He waited until Ivan had completed several rounds, then stopped him and let him fall to all fours.

Dixie brought out some chunks of sirloin she had gotten from Miss Clara and fed the bear. "You did fine, Ivan," she said. "I'm proud of you. Where *is* your father, David?"

"I don't know," he said. " He told me to come and work with the bears some. He said he had an important meeting."

Clara took off her apron and laid it down, then turned to Gregori Malkovitch.

They were inside the cook tent. "Are you sure we can't just talk here?" she asked. "I've got to get the evening meal started."

Gregori had an odd look on his face. "No," he said, "it is too . . . what you say . . . public here."

"Well, all right. We can go outside somewhere, but at a circus nearly every place is public!"

The Russian stepped aside for her as she left the tent, and they started to walk. He looked this way and that, and then he pointed to the open field beyond where the trailers were parked. "That is a good place," he said.

Clara was puzzled. She walked along beside him, glancing at him from time to time, but he said nothing more. Finally, they had reached the farthest corner of the field. She considered all the open space about them and said, "This certainly looks private enough."

Gregori looked around, too. He took off the hat that he almost always wore, and the wind blew his reddish brown hair freely. "*Da,*" he said. "It looks a little like the steppes in my country."

"Do you miss Russia a lot, Gregori?"

"No, not so much now. It is hard times

there, you understand. Communism has gone, but something may come along that is worse. It is a hard place to live. Not like this country."

"You like it here, don't you?"

"*Da.* I came for my children's sake. Not so much for me."

"You have lovely children."

"You never had any children?"

"I had one. A little girl." Clara looked at the ground for a moment. Then she lifted her eyes. "She died when she was two. I miss her every day."

Gregori stared at her with surprise on his face. Then he reached out unexpectedly and took her hand. His voice was soft as he said, "I am so sorry."

Clara finally looked up at him and smiled. "But you know what I say. She's not lost, because I know where she is."

"*Da,* she is with Jesus."

Clara laughed at his remembering. She had expected him to drop her hand, but he did not. At last she decided to say, "You're holding my hand, Gregori."

"Is this improper in this country? I do not know the customs here."

Clara was flustered. She did not know

what to say. She looked into the tall Russian's clear blue eyes and said, "I suppose a little hand holding isn't frowned upon much these days."

Gregori smiled slightly. Then he suddenly leaned over and kissed her hand.

Clara was stunned, and, for the first time in many years, the big woman felt herself blush. For once, loud Clara Rendell, who was never short of something to say, had nothing to say!

"I have thought much about what Reverend Sullivan says about being born again. And I have studied the Bible that you gave me with the red marks underlining the words." He looked off into the blue sky where white clouds were floating. He was quiet for so long that Clara wondered what was happening.

But then Gregori Malkovitch turned back to her, and she saw tears in his eyes. "Last night, after the children were asleep, I got out of my bed, Clara. I got on my knees, and I asked the Lord Jesus to come into my heart—and He did!"

"Oh, Gregori, what wonderful news! I'm so glad!" She reached out to him then, and this time she held *his* hand.

An expression of peace came into the Russian's eyes, and he said, "Clara, you are a fine woman. As fine as my wife. I've been wrong to let the memory of her become so big. I have not been fair to my children—or to other people. But it will be different now."

"How will things be different, Gregori?"

"From now on, I'm going to live for God." He looked at her intently then and said, "Will you help me?"

Clara's eyes filled with tears. This big man, so far away from his homeland, had such a hopeful spirit. He had been confused and unhappy, but now she knew that things would be better.

"Yes, Gregori, I'll help you," she whispered.

For several weeks Dixie was totally happy. Now she was giving signing lessons to all three Malkovitches. They spent almost every evening together after the final performance. Sometimes they had class in the morning too. Every day Dixie found herself growing closer to the bears.

"I love Ivan almost as much as I love Stripes," she told Aunt Sarah one day as they were eating breakfast.

"Well, that's a lot." Sarah smiled. "You've always loved that tiger."

"And I always will. But Ivan is so gentle. He's not as smart as Stripes, but I love him all the same."

She would have said more, but suddenly there was a loud banging on the door.

Sarah blinked with astonishment. "All right! All right! Don't break the door down!" she said. When she opened it, David Malkovitch was standing on the step. His face was troubled.

"What's wrong, David? Is something wrong with one of the bears?"

"No, it's Papa!" David said desperately. "He's hurt his back."

"Is it serious?" Sarah asked.

"I don't know. He has hurt it before. The last time he was in bed for a long time. I thought he was never going to get up."

"Well, I'm not a people doctor, David, but we'll go see him anyway."

David looked at Dixie with relief in his eyes.

Dixie walked beside him on the way to the Malkovitch trailer, and she could tell that he was worried. "Don't worry. It'll be all right," she told him, but he did not answer.

When they arrived they found Katy sitting beside her father. He was lying on the bed, and his face behind his beard was pale.

"You should not have bothered our friends, David."

"Nonsense," Sarah said. "That's what friends are for. Tell me what happened. Did you fall?"

"No. It came last night. I did nothing. I cannot understand what it is. Just the way it was last time. That's been over two years now."

"What did the doctors say then, Gregori?"

"Something about a . . . a disk. They wanted to operate, but they said I would be paralyzed if it did not work. So I just waited and waited, and finally it got well."

"It'll be well again," Sarah said, "but we'll have to get you to a doctor."

Gregori looked up and protested. "No, I have so little money, and if we cannot do the act, we will have nothing."

Dixie stepped closer and put her hand on the sick man's arm. "God can do anything, Mr. Malkovitch. You can always trust Him."

But Gregori Malkovitch was worried indeed. He had two children and only one means of making a living. Now that he was flat on his back, he'd suddenly remembered how hard it was when he had been out of work for almost a year that other time. He told them all that, then looked at Dixie and tried to smile. "I will ask all of my friends in the church to pray for me."

"Exactly," Sarah said. "And they will. Now you lie there and don't worry about a thing. I'll go make the arrangements for the doctor. Really, don't worry. I am sure I can get the circus to take care of the medical bills."

Gregori Malkovitch looked over at his children, and though he was in pain he managed a smile. "We must believe God, my children."

"Yes, Papa," David said.

Katy, who had been watching her father's lips, turned to Dixie, and Dixie signed her father's words.

Katy immediately signed back, "We will trust the good Lord God."

12
A NEW BEAR ACT

It is good of you to help me, Clara," Gregori Malkovitch said. She had placed a heating pad under him, and he looked up at her with a grateful expression. "It has been a long time since anyone took such good care of me."

Clara flushed and smiled down at the big Russian. "I thought at one time I would be a nurse," she murmured. "Are you any better at all today, Gregori?"

"Yes, I am." He nodded. "I can already tell the difference. It is not going to be like the last time."

"Whatever happens, God's going to take care of you. A lot of people are praying."

"I never knew," Gregori said, "that it would be like this to be a child of God. Why, the circus church is like a big family."

"I'm glad you think of us like that. That's the way a church should be."

But reaching up to push his hair back from his forehead, Gregori looked troubled again. "I know you said that Christians are not to worry. Still, I can't help thinking about what's going to happen to my act. If I don't perform, I won't get paid. I suppose it is a holdover from my days in Russia— things were so hard there. And I don't want to go into debt."

"It will be all right," Clara assured him. "God knows what He is doing. He will take care of everything."

"But David has never done the act alone. And even if he had, it still takes two, one for Ivan and one for Ilona."

"It will be all right," Clara repeated. "We'll just pray right now that God will make a way."

Dixie and David stood together watching the Malkovitch bears.

"It's wonderful how Miss Clara has come to help with Papa," David said.

Dixie glanced at him slyly. "You know, I think that they might get married some-day. Would that bother you?"

"No. Not at all," David said at once. "She's such a good woman. And it would be nice to have a mama again. Especially it would be good for Katy. Miss Clara already loves her so much."

Dixie admired Ivan again and said, "Ivan's such a nice bear. And so clever. It's a shame that you can't go ahead and do the act yourself."

"Oh, I believe I *could* do it, although I never have. Not the real thing. And not all by myself. Papa wants me to wait until I'm older."

"But you already know all the commands. And the bears are used to you."

"That's true." David nodded. "But I still can't control both of them at the same time."

Dixie gave Ivan a small piece of meat from the supply she had brought along. He grunted and nuzzled her for more, which she gave him. Then she patted his massive head and said, "You're a good old bear, Ivan. I bet you can ride a bicycle better than most kids I know."

Later that night, David decided to have a talk with his father. "I think you should let me do the act, Papa."

Mr. Malkovitch disagreed at once. "No, it is too much for you, David." He sat up slowly and painfully. "This sickness will not be like the last time. I'll be out of this bed very soon. Then we will do the act together."

"The doctor said you shouldn't get out too quickly. It would make you worse. And he said it might still be a month before you will be well!"

"I cannot help it. I have to work sooner than that. We have to put on the act."

"But, Papa—"

A knock sounded, and David looked around in surprise. "Who can that be?"

"Go see."

David, however, nodded at Katy and pointed to the door.

His little sister went at once and opened it. Looking down the corridor of the trailer, David saw Dixie Morris on the step.

Dixie greeted her, then, when Katy motioned for her to come in, she stepped inside. "I need to see your papa," she said, signing at the same time.

Katy came running back and signed this quickly, but David had heard.

"Do you feel like seeing Dixie, Papa?"

"She's probably come to see you."

But Dixie called, "No, I'd like to see you, Mr. Malkovitch. Can I come back?"

"Of course. Come."

Dixie came and stood beside the bed, and David could see that her eyes were shining. She was also fidgeting nervously. "Mr. Malkovitch, I've got something to tell you."

David looked at her, puzzled. He knew that she was excited, but what about? "What is it, Dixie?"

"I've got an idea. Mr. Malkovitch, why don't you let David and me do your act with the bears?"

"You!" Gregori exclaimed. "That is impossible!"

"Nothing is impossible for God," Dixie said firmly.

"Yes, I believe that very well—but some things are impossible for *little girls.*"

"It's not impossible for us at all. Maybe we couldn't do *all* the act, but I can do the simple things, and David can show me all that I need to do. I've watched your act every night, Mr. Malkovitch. I know everything you do. And Ivan already obeys everything I tell him. Doesn't he, David?"

"She's very good with the bears, Papa,"

143

David assured his father. "Maybe it would be all right. Ivan likes Dixie so much, I think he'd follow any of her commands. And I could handle Ilona."

"No, no, no, no! It would be too dangerous, and your aunt would never consent, Dixie! For that matter, *I* will not consent!"

What followed then was an argument that lasted for half an hour. Dixie kept insisting that it could be done. David's father kept saying that their doing the bear act alone would be too dangerous.

At last Dixie said, "Mr. Malkovitch, I know I'm very young, and so is David, but somehow I think God has put me here to help you. Will you do this much: let David and me rehearse, and then, if it doesn't go well, then we won't do it—"

"But if it does, you will insist, won't you?" he asked.

"No, but it would be nice."

At last Mr. Malkovitch said, "All right. All right. You can *rehearse,* but it must go well. And David, you must tell me the truth. I know you like Dixie, but it must be more than that."

"I promise, Papa. We'll go try it right now."

On their way to rehearse with the bears, Dixie ran by the cook tent. There she found Miss Clara peeling potatoes, and Dixie explained the situation. "You have to go over and talk to Mr. Malkovitch, Miss Clara."

"Wait, wait. I'm not sure I should. Besides, you've got to see how your practice goes. And first, we'd have to talk to your aunt."

"No, we can talk to Aunt Sarah later. First, *Mr. Malkovitch* has to agree. You convince him, and then I can talk Aunt Sarah into letting me do the act."

"You're pretty sure of that, are you?"

Dixie grinned impudently. "I think I can. Now, you do your stuff with Mr. Malkovitch, and I'll do mine with Aunt Sarah."

That night the circus performance went as usual, except for when it came time for the Malkovitch's Trained Bears.

Then the ringmaster came forward with an announcement. "And now, ladies and gentlemen, we have a first in circus history! You are well aware that trained bear acts can be very dangerous! Gregori Malkovitch, who brought his family and his bears from Russia, is world renowned. But Mr. Malkovitch has suffered a slight illness, and tonight in his place we have two new stars in the circus world! For tonight the Malkovitch Trained Bears will be directed by David Malkovitch, eleven-year-old son of Gregori Malkovitch, and Dixie Morris, ten-year-old niece of Sarah Logan, our great veterinarian! I ask you to give a good hand to the newest stars in the firmament of the circus world!"

Dixie and David had been waiting behind the flap of the curtain. David was wearing a Cossack uniform, black boots with baggy trousers stuffed inside, a blouse fastened by a black belt, and a black hat. Ilona waited beside him.

Dixie wore the same, except that she wore a skirt instead of black trousers. She whispered, "Come on, Ivan, there's our cue." She glanced over at David.

He winked at her and said, "Let's go, Dixie."

They led the bears out under the spotlights, and for a second Dixie almost lost her courage. *What if I can't do this?* she thought. *It's one thing to rehearse when it's quiet, but now—in front of all these people and with the band playing—it's hard! I might fail.* She whispered a quick prayer. "Lord, let me do this right."

Then for some reason she thought of a verse that Aunt Sarah had taught their Sunday school class—*Whether, then, you eat or drink or whatever you do, do all to the glory of God.* And Dixie added to her prayer, "Let me do this act with Ivan to the glory of God."

As the performance went on, Dixie almost forgot they were in front of thousands of people. Ivan behaved perfectly, and she praised him and slipped him a bite of delicious meat after he did every trick.

When the act was over, Dixie and David and the bears received a tremendous ovation. Then the ringmaster came running up. He hugged Dixie and shook David's hand and had them take more bows.

When they had taken the bears out from under the Big Top and back to their cages, Dixie threw her arms around Ivan and hugged him with all her might.

Suddenly the big bear reared up on his hind legs, and Dixie found herself dangling from his neck. He seemed to be patting her back, but she guessed he was actually searching for more goodies.

"Put me down, Ivan," she protested, laughing. When he did, she gave him all the goodies she had left in her pocket.

At that moment Darla came by, and she had a frozen look on her face. "I guess you think you're something, don't you?"

"I think Ivan is something," Dixie said.

Darla sniffed. "Anybody can waltz around the ring with a silly old bear! You ought to try something really hard some-time."

But Dixie was accustomed to Darla's ways. She merely laughed and said, "Why don't you come here and let Ivan pick you up? Come on, Ivan, this young lady wants to be hugged."

Darla screamed as the massive bear lumbered toward her. "Keep that beast away from me!" she yelled. She turned and fled.

Dixie reached up and patted Ivan's shaggy side. "That's a good old bear," she told him.

13

THIS ISN'T RUSSIA

Rev. Mooey Sullivan sang with enthusiasm as he led the first two hymns. After those were over, he winked at his wife, who was playing the portable organ. Then he looked up at his congregation of circus people seated on the center ring grandstand of the Big Top.

"We have some special music for you this morning. If I were a ringmaster, I would say, 'Now for the first time under the Big Top we have a new act.'" Mooey looked around at the surprised faces. Then he said, "For our solo today I've asked Miss Dixie Morris to come and sing. And I've asked her good friend and fellow bear trainer, David Malkovitch, to sign in the American Sign Language for his sister, Katy. Come along, young folks, and give us all a treat."

Dixie had been surprised when Mooey asked her to do this. She talked to her aunt about it, and Aunt Sarah said right away, "That's a fine idea. It will give you a chance to sing, and it will be a good thing for David and Katy. They need to come out of themselves."

Dixie stood by the organ and glanced at David coming to stand beside her. There on the front row was Katy. She was sitting beside her father, who was wearing his blue suit and white shirt, and on her other side sat Clara Rendell, who had on a new pink dress.

Dixie swallowed hard. Then she nodded to Mrs. Sullivan, who began to play. She sang one of her favorite songs, "What a Friend We Have in Jesus."

As Dixie sang in her clear, sweet voice, David made the signs. She watched him out of the corner of her eye and saw that he was doing it perfectly. Then she looked over at Katy. The little girl was smiling broadly. Miss Clara's arm went around Katy, and over *her* arm Gregori Malkovitch placed his. He had a pair of crutches beside him, but he had insisted on coming to hear this service.

As Dixie finished the song, she thought, *It's so wonderful that God is able to do these things.* She stepped down from the small platform the organ sat on and was surprised when David put out his hand to help her. "You did fine, David."

"I was pretty scared," he said.

"You didn't have to be. And did you see Katy? I think she understood most all the words of the song."

"I'm sure glad you talked me into learning how to sign. It's different at home now, being able to talk to Katy. And now she can ask for what she wants. I believe you must be an angel." He smiled as he said this and raised one eyebrow.

"Well, I'm not, and nobody ever called me that," Dixie said. "But I wish you'd tell Aunt Sarah. She sometimes isn't quite sure I'm angelic."

The Royal Circus moved on to Texas, and while there, exactly three weeks after Dixie's solo, Gregori Malkovitch and David were baptized. It was a beautiful baptism. They used a large tank that the clowns used for part of their act. It gave Dixie a great thrill to see Mooey Sullivan lowering them into the water. And when they both came up, all the congregation applauded just as if they had done a difficult stunt.

Gregori said, as soon as he stepped out of the tank, "Today I am a happy man. I thank God for bringing me to America with my family, and I thank Him for letting me have people who care for me. But especially I am glad the Savior found me."

There was no afternoon performance that day, so Mr. Malkovitch took all of the older boys and girls to Six Flags. He was not able to walk a great deal even yet, but he and Miss Clara sat while the children enjoyed the rides all day and ate everything they could hold.

After they had gone back to the circus for the evening show, he kept telling everybody, "We will eat a meal tonight after the performance—but one that Clara will not have to cook."

Miss Clara was puzzled by all this. "Whatever do you mean, Gregori?"

"You will see," he said mysteriously.

The rest of the circus people were all curious, too.

After the show, everyone gathered in the cook tent, where they murmured in amazement at seeing food on two long tables and a staff of waiters and waitresses ready to serve them.

"I hired all this from a restaurant," Mr. Malkovitch announced when everyone got still. "Now, we will have the blessing, and then we will eat. Pastor Mooey, you pray."

Mooey prayed, and then they ate as if they were starving.

Midway through the meal, Gregori Malkovitch got up and called out in his deep, booming voice, "May I have your attention?"

Everyone looked his way, and silence fell over the tent. "I have an announcement to make." He looked very pleased with himself. Reaching down to Miss Clara, who sat at his right, he put a hand on her shoulder. "I wish to announce that Clara and I are engaged."

"Hooray!" Dixie cried, and she saw that David and Katy were very happy, too.

Everyone applauded except Miss Clara. She stood up, and her eyes flashed. "You announced our engagement without proposing?" she exclaimed.

Mr. Malkovitch was taken aback. He mumbled, "Why, Clara, this is the way we do it in Russia."

"Well, we're not in Russia," Clara Rendell said. "We're in Texas! And if you want to marry me, you'll have to come courting."

"Courting? What is courting?"

A laugh went up from everyone, and Dixie called out, "I'll tell you all about it, Mr. Malkovitch. It's not hard."

Everybody laughed again, but Mr. Malkovitch was crushed. "Are you angry, Clara?" he asked rather pitifully.

"No, I'm not angry. I'm very flattered, but I'm going to be courted before I will agree to marry you."

"I will courting you tomorrow," he said, and the circus people laughed once more at his error in English.

Then Katy got up from her place on the other side of her father. She came around to Miss Clara and signed something.

The cook turned to Dixie. "What did she say?"

"She said, 'I want you to marry my daddy, and then we'll all be a family.'"

Miss Clara turned back and threw an arm around Katy, almost lifting her off the floor. Then she reached out and grabbed David, sitting next to her, and hugged him with her free arm. Finally, she looked at Mr.

Malkovitch. She said, "Well, you can court me *after* we're married, I suppose."

"Hooray!" David yelled and threw his Russian hat high in the air.

Dixie felt the tears coming. *Why do I always cry when I'm happy?* she thought. *I ought to cry just when I'm sad.*

After all that, the engagement party went on. Everybody said it was a great success.

Later that evening when Dixie and her aunt were back in the Airstream, Dixie said, "I'm going by and say good night to Ivan, Aunt Sarah."

"All right, but you come home soon. You've had a busy day."

Dixie ran to the bear cage, where she found, to her surprise, that someone was there.

"What are you doing, Eric?" she asked.

"Nothing!"

"What have you got in your hand?"

"That's none of your business!" Eric said. But then he grinned. "Look how mad he gets when I show him this and won't give him any." He held an open jar of something up to the bars of the bear cage.

Ivan tried to reach it but could not, and he began to whine and grumble.

Suddenly David appeared. "What's going on here?" he asked. "What are you doing with my bear?"

"See," Eric said happily. "He likes this honey, but I'm not giving him any of it."

David and Dixie must have both had the same thought. "You *like* to tease, don't you?" David said. "You like to tease people, and you like to tease animals. It makes you feel good."

"It's fun. Ivan's just a dumb old bear. He's not near as smart as one of our horses."

"You like to tease, but other people don't like to be teased, Eric," Dixie said. "Neither do bears."

All at once David grabbed the honey jar. He handed it to Dixie, then wrapped his arms around Eric. "Pour it all over him, Dixie. All over his head!" he commanded.

Dixie giggled. She began to pour the liquid honey over Eric's hair. It ran down his face. It ran into his ears.

Eric, of course, began screaming at the top of his lungs. "Let me go! Let me go!"

"Sure, we'll let you go, but first you've got to be nice to Ivan. You offered him the honey, and now he gets it. That's only fair."

David pushed Eric close to the bars of Ivan's cage. Holding him by the back of the neck, he shoved Eric's head right between two of them.

Ivan at once began lapping at the honey. The bear's long red tongue licked across Eric's face again and again, and he rumbled deep in his throat, a sign that he was pleased.

Then Dixie said, "That's enough, David. I think he's learned his lesson."

Eric jerked away as David released him. He yelled, "I'll get you for this!" and then went running off, his face still sticky with the honey that Ivan had not been able to lick off.

"I hate it when people are mean and tease animals," David said.

"So do I, but I really don't think Eric will do it again. Not soon anyway."

Dixie reached through the bars and patted Ivan. "You're a good old bear," she said.

Then she remembered. "Oh—oh. Aunt Sarah said I had to get home."

"More signing lessons tomorrow?"

"If you want to."

"I sure do." David Malkovitch took a deep breath, then he put out his hand.

Surprised, Dixie took it.

And then he said something in Russian.

"What does that mean?"

"I won't tell you all of it." He grinned. "But part of it means, 'Dixie Morris, you're the finest girl I know.'"

Dixie blushed and looked down at the ground. Then she smiled at David and said, "When you come over tomorrow, I'll make us some candied popcorn and some hot chocolate. It'll probably make you sick, though."

"I'll be there."

Dixie gave Ivan one more pat on his sticky nose. After that she ran off toward the Airstream trailer, happy that God had let her help a family that needed help.

Moody Press, a ministry of the Moody Bible Institute, is designed for education, evangelization, and edification. If we may assist you in knowing more about Christ and the Christian life, please write us without obligation: Moody Press, c/o MLM, Chicago, Illinois 60610.